valley of the blind

"In the Valley of the Blind, only love is blind"

Written by David Criswell

valley of the blind

Written by David Criswell

Inspired by Desiderius Erasmus, H.G. Wells, H. Rider Haggard, John Henry
Newton, and the parables of Jesus Christ

Cover design by David Criswell, from a painting by Ivan Aivazovsky

FORTRESS

ADONAI
PRESS

Dedication:

For Greeta.
Thank you for helping me with my *bahut bura Hindi*.

Table of Contents

1 – The Valley of Shangri La

To have a debate, there must be a question. Does a gardener debate with a writer? Does an artist debate with a mechanic? Can a doctor debate a poet? Or a soldier debate a nurse? And yet the Darwinist not only debates the Newtonian Creationist, but denies there is a question to debate at all!

"Science and religion have nothing to do with one another," Raja used to tell his friend all the time.

To which, his friend, James Milton, would invariably reply, "then why do the two so often conflict with one another?"

"Because religion doesn't know its place," was the usual retort.

Such were the invariable arguments of James Milton and Raja Sinha. Their debates were understandable, for Milton was a missionary and Raja a professor of science. People were neither surprised nor amused by their constant arguments. Rather it was their friendship which astounded people. This was something most people did not understand. Indeed, perhaps even Raja and James did not understand it, but their mothers did.

Raja was a self professed skeptic. He looked down upon religion, having seen caste war-fare and religious riots throughout his childhood in his native country of India, Raja had developed a distaste for all religion. Science was the solution to man's problems, and this was not his opinion, it was a *fact*, or so he assumed.

Milton too called himself a skeptic, but he was a different kind of skeptic. He would often remind

Raja that to be skeptical of whether or not maggots, slugs, and cockroaches were our distant cousins is no less skeptical than doubting Isaac Newton's principle of First Cause or the Prime Mover. In Milton's world he had seen atheists like Joseph Stalin and Mao Tse-Tung butcher more people than all the religions of human history combined; a fact of which he constantly reminded Raja. He learned how Hitler had used science to make genocide like an assembly line. He saw how doctors would use drugs to kill, rather than to heal, and how psychiatrists in old Russia made belief in God a neurosis to be treated with electroshock therapy and lobotomies.

"But now psychiatry is much more advanced," Raja would reply.

"More antiseptic you mean. Do you realize that psychoactive drugs do the exact same thing to the brain that electroshock therapy and lobotomies did?"

Such were their debates, which drove many of their friends away simply out of a desire to avoid listening. They simply could not understand their friendship, but mothers understand what we do not. They understood that Raja and Milton valued each other's friendship precisely because they liked to be challenged in their beliefs. They were both skeptics of a sort. If Thomas Jefferson's acceptance of Nature's God is fact, then Raja preferred nature whereas Milton preferred God. The two are interrelated, but different fields; science and religion.

Now I only bring up this topic because it is necessary to understand why two such men would not only be friends, but why both men would be scaling the Himalayan Mountains in search of a valley in which neither of them particularly believed existed!

It seems that every culture has a legend of a paradise city. In Europe Thomas More's myth of the lost island of Utopia brought heaven to earth. Some say Plato's Republic envisioned such a society. China had Tao Hua Yuanl. In India it is a Valley called Shangri La, hidden somewhere in the Himalayas. Such myths were completely rejected by both Raja and Milton, and yet rumors of a valley literally hidden from the air intrigued the men. It is said that planes cannot see into the valley because sheer cliff faces disguise the valley from too far in the air. To bring any plane too close would be too dangerous because of the swirling winds which also make it impossible to send helicopters into that region.

How then could such a valley be reached? And if it is so impossible to reach, then how could anyone have ever been there to know what lies within? Raja and Milton looked upon the stories as akin to the Yeti or Abominable Snowman legend, and yet there seemed no doubt that a valley did indeed lie hidden somewhere within that region. A close examination of maps and aerial photos show that there was a small area which had never been charted. That was their excuse. Valley of Shangri La or not, they would chart the valley which had never been seen before, and should they encounter any Yeti along the way ... well, that would be a bonus, or so they joked.

They stopped at a Buddhist monastery built high upon the western side of the mountains, laying between the city of Lucknow, Uttar Pradesh, in India and the Nepali city of Kathmandu. The monastery lay just inside the border of Nepal, so Raja was quite relieved to find that the monks never asked them for their passports, as they had come through India and were technically illegally trespassing within Nepal. Milton, on the other hand, laughed off Raja's worries.

"Monks are not politicians and could care less," he said, but little did he realize that these monks were political in a different sense. A fact neither Raja nor Milton would become conscious of for some time to come.

Nevertheless, the monks politely pointed the way, and that way seemed to be up.

"Up?" asked the bewildered Raja.

The monks simply nodded.

Apparently, they were told that the valley can only be reached by scaling sheer cliffs of ice and then descending down the other side, and yet the monks, polite as they were, made many ominous warnings.

"The way is dangerous. None have scaled those cliffs and survived," they warned.

Since neither Raja nor Milton were expert mountain climbers, let alone ice climbers, they should have heeded the warning, but they were somewhat suspicious of the monks. They believed what they were told, but with a caution. The monks clearly did not appreciate intruders and fortune seekers. Were they the guardians of this mythical valley? If they were, might they not be pointing them toward certain death, giving the ominous warnings as a means to appease their guilty consciences?

These were the thoughts of Raja and Milton as they scaled up the mountains. With each step Milton became more and more tired, and these thoughts became more and more acute. Were they risking their lives for nothing? Was the valley even in the direction they were traveling? Why were the monks so eager to point the way if they did not want them to find the valley? Milton was exhausted, but Raja wanted to press onward.

"Not until we reach the top. Then we can rest."

Raja was the more experienced climber, but neither was prepared properly. They had not even brought breathing masks. After all, they were expecting to descend into a valley, not scale a mountain top. Likewise, their supplies were shockingly limited. Raja felt that they should not be weighed down unnecessarily and had been assured that the valley was not more than a day's journey from the monastery, so they left most of their supplies with the monks and traveled with only three days worth of food and water.

The real peril was in the steep sheer cliff face itself, made of solid ice it seemed. Raja led the way. This only made sense since Raja had more experience. If Milton fell, Raja could pull him up as their cords were firmly attached to one another, but if the top man fell, the jolt would surely pull the second man down as well. Mountain climbers must rely on one another in such instances, and these two friends, for all their differences, were willing to place their life in the other's hands. Nonetheless, there are times that nothing can save a man. There are times when

God has predetermined an action. The Hindus call it destiny or *kisma*. The Buddhist call it fate. Christians call it something far more, for predestination is neither *kisma* nor fate. Each integrates its own theology with the concept, but that concept is simply this; there was nothing Raja could do to stop what was to happen. And moreover, the consequences of what was to happen would not be known, nor felt by him, for ten years, and yet the consequences would affect the rest of Raja's life, and change the course of a lost civilization.

Raja had finally dug his pick into the top of the cliff and pulled himself up, when he crawled forward a few paces and rolled over on his back to rest. The cord still tugged tight as Milton had not yet made it to the top.

No sooner had Raja closed his eyes to rest than he felt a tight snap and tug. He was sliding toward the cliff's edge as the cord had gone taut and pulled at him. Milton had fallen. Raja quickly regained his senses and dug his feet into the snow and ice, before reaching the ledge. He then grabbed a hold of the cord and began to pull Milton up. He did not even bother speaking; that was useless. He concentrated on pulling Milton up. There would be time to talk later, or so he assumed.

As Raja pulled back on the cord, he found himself falling backward into the snow. This was not because he lost grip on the rope, but because the cord had snapped. Perhaps it caught on one of the sharp ice ledges. It didn't matter. There was no one at the other end of the rope.

"Jimmmm!" cried Raja, but there was no answer. The cliff was a sheer drop, and Raja could barely even see over the edge. He repeated his cries to no avail. He remembered no ledges upon which Milton might safely have landed, and if he had landed safely somewhere, he was not answering. Worse yet, there was no signal for Raja to call out for help with his cell phone; a fact he knew beforehand. By the time he returned to the monks, all hope was lost. A token search party and fly over was sent out by both Nepal and India, but it was believed that the snow and ice had buried the remains. Milton was gone.

2 – An Unexpected Visitor

Ten years had passed since the events upon the Himalayan mountain. Raja had never forgotten his old friend, and he missed the intellectual challenges that Milton once supplied to stimulate his brain. Now all he had was his students, who seldom even cared who was right or who was wrong, for that would imply that there was such a thing as right and wrong; a concept unpopular in public education in America today.

On this day Raja was initiating a new class. As he did with all his classes he would begin by challenging the students' beliefs. He would make sure they understood the difference in science and "superstition." Of course, every now and again, a student would challenge Raja's beliefs. This was something Milton used to do all the time, but Raja despised it when a student did so. There was a pecking order, a hierarchy (although Raja would never use such a word reminiscent of the medieval church), and students were at the bottom of that hierarchy.

Most classes were made up of a body of students who inevitably followed a pattern. There were the Kiss-up artists, the Worshippers, the Smart-alecks, the Know-it-alls, the Party Animals, the I Don't Cares, and the Why Am I Heres.

The Kiss-up artists were those who pretended to love the professor and hinge on his every word, yet cannot remember any of those words come test time. They flatter the professors and befriend them and then hope that the professors like them enough to pass them even though they clearly never pay attention in class.

The Worshippers are a sincere variant of the Kiss-up artists, differing only in that they really do believe every word the professor says, no matter how stupid. They parrot the professors words without thinking and frequently talk like a walking textbook as unaware of what they just said as the listener is of what they spoke. The Worshippers frequently become teachers aides and do well in the academia, but when they venture out into the real world, they find themselves living under a bridge somewhere; hence they return to school on a scholarship and become career students, or worse ... professors.

The Smart-aleck frequently sits in the back, afraid to be seen, but constantly heard. He likes to take jibes at the professor and crack jokes, which may or may not be funny, although none are ever funny in the professor's eyes. The Smart-aleck is a variant of the Know-it-all.

The Know-it-all likes to challenge the professor, but doesn't like to be challenged himself. He always has an answer for every question, whether he knows what he is talking about or not. Professors particularly despise this class of students for the primary reason that the professor himself is a Know-it-all. As is common to human nature, we hate most in others what is the most common sin in ourselves. The one who calls others hypocrites all the time is most often a hypocrite in his own heart. The one who frequently calls others racists, is a bigot in his own heart. What we see in others, is too often what lies in our own hearts. With this in mind, let me say that the reader is very insightful and intelligent.

The Party Animal is, of course, what you would expect. For the professor he is not really a problem, because he is usually asleep throughout class and does not provide a distraction. Failing the Party Animal is also easy for it suits both the professor and the student, who now has an excuse to attend more parties over the course of yet another year paid for by his father.

The I Don't Cares and Why Am I Heres comprise two different breeds of the same species. They attend because it is better than getting a job, but they have no real interest in pursuing a career in whatever their major may be. Consequently these two groups often evolve into Party Animals or Know-it-alls.

Now in Raja's new class, it was not hard to tell which was which, but this semester he had a particularly troublesome Know-it-all, or perhaps he was only a Smart-aleck. Raja wasn't quite sure yet, but Raja was becoming particularly annoyed with this one. Not so much because of his remarks, so much as the fact that Raja was unable to answer the remarks.

"As a student of science," began Raja's usual introduction, "I do not believe in anything that I cannot see and observe."

"You mean you don't believe in gravity?" inquired the Smart-aleck.

Frowning somewhat, and ignoring obvious chuckles from the class, Raja explained, "I cannot see gravity, but I can see its result. Science is based on cause and effect. For every action there is a cause.

You drop an object, it falls. The cause of that is called gravity." So far Raja Sihna was holding his ground quite well.

"So you believe in the First Cause? Newton's Prime Mover?" asked one of the religious students (there is one in every science class for some reason, although Raja could never understand why).

"The First Cause, as you call it, would imply a supernatural process. Can you show me the chemical equation for God, or put His magic under a microscope?" Raja replied.

To which the Smart-aleck, disguising his voice slightly (although Raja knew exactly who was speaking), "So you can see gravity under a microscope? Will we learn the chemical equation for gravity today chief?"

Raja gave the student a firm look, despite knowing that it seldom worked to silence the Smart-aleck. Fortunately, he was saved by another query, "What about feelings? Do scientists not feel love?"

Naturally, this question came from a young woman, so Raja merely smiled, and replied, "Well, feelings are rather subjective. They involve bodily chemistry and neurochemistry in the brain. Physiology is what we call it, although psychiatry struggles to find the balance between cause and effect. This one problem with psychiatry. Until it is able to distinguish between etiology and physiology, it remains a bit of a pseudo-science."

The students looked at one another a bit bewildered, when the Know-it-all bravely spoke up,

"Would you have believed in dinosaurs before the science of paleontology?"

"Of course not; no more than I believe in sea monsters or dragons, but now science has advanced to the point to where we can know that dinosaurs once existed." Part of Raja knew he was loosing the argument. This is why, after observing the faces of the students, he breathed a small sigh and reluctantly made a small concession, in hopes it might silence the students, "Look, I know where you are going. Let me just say, I am not an atheist. Atheism is as stubborn and rigid and emotional as these religious nuts. I guess I am just an agnostic. God may exist, but I just don't care."

Student expressions ranged from indescribable to descriptions I choose not to describe. Some laughed. Some were angry. Some nodded agreeably. Some were asleep and didn't hear the comment at all. Raja was about to follow up the comment when the door opened. An elderly lady poked her head in, saying, "Doctor? I hope I am not interrupting."

In the back the Smart-aleck could be heard in a muffled voice, "not at all. *Please* come in," with an emphatic emphasis upon "please."

The elderly lady did just that, and handed Raja a note. She then quietly turned around and left without saying another word. Lest one think this is odd behavior, the reader should be aware that secretaries are supposed to write notes so that they can leave them without interrupting the professor at all, if possible. She was, therefore, a little embarrassed at having done so after the mocking comment from the student hidden in the back of the classroom.

Raja read the note, and then put it in his shirt pocket. He looked up at the class, somewhat frustrated, and said, "I am sure you will be happy to know that I dismissing class early today, but ..." The words were not even out of his mouth before a few students were starting out the door. There seemed a general sigh of relief from some, and joy from others. As the students made their way to the door, Raja finally finished his sentence, "but there will be a quiz tomorrow." Now Raja was quite deliberate in his delay in speaking these final words, for he secretly wanted to punish those who had darted for the door so quickly, but his repressed joy at seeing those students miss this vital piece of information was countered by the fact that the class Smart-aleck was still sitting in his chair at the back of the class chatting with someone else. The Smart-aleck heard about the quiz but some of the students on the front row did not. Somehow there seemed to be no justice in the world, or at least that is how Raja felt.

Now Raja's feelings were not entirely because of the class. He had awoken this morning rather grumpy to start the day, and the note which had been handed to him only added to the frustration of the day. This despite the fact that there was nothing particularly sinister or unsettling in the note. It read simply:

"A distraught man was insistent upon seeing you. When we informed him that you would not be available until this afternoon, he said he had another important appointment and could not wait but left a message. He said:

'Tell him that I will await him tonight in the Hotel Dallas
Restaurant
at 5 o'clock'

At the bottom of the note was the man's name. It was James Milton.

So Raja sat with mixed emotions. It is not unsettling to find that a long lost friend is alive, but it did bring up many questions in Raja's mind; not just the obvious one, like how he survived or where he has been for the past ten years, but even more subtle curiosities like what was the important appointment that usurps his reunion with Raja? Why was he staying at the Hotel Dallas when his family still lived in the Dallas suburb of Plano, Texas? This is how Raja's mind worked. Small details sometimes came before the obvious. Sometimes, as the old saying goes, he could not see the forest for examining the trees. This had always been Milton's estimation of Raja. Raja was caught up in the small details so that he could not see the bigger picture. He put everything under a microscope so that he could not even remember what the specimen looked like before he placed it there.

It was Francis Bacon who had said, "A little bit of science distances a man from God, but a lot of science brings man back to Him." Milton always believed that Raja would come back to God, but for now it was Milton that had come back to Raja, and the latter was torn between curiosity, joy, and even a little anger. Why had his friend been missing for ten years? Milton's answers would be essential in Raja's decision whether to hug or hit his long lost friend.

The Hotel Dallas was by no means a luxury hotel, but neither was it a budget hotel. There was a piano in the restaurant on a small stage which was empty for the present. The tables were nice and the cloths decorated with dozens of outlines of the State of Texas. Texas, you see, is a proud state. It was an individual nation before ever joining the Union. In fact, every time a Democrat is elected President of the United States there are quiet whispers among many in Texas that joining the Union was a mistake. Those whispers, however, disappear when a Republican from Texas is elected President.

The restaurant was empty except for Milton, who was sitting at a table in the corner of the restaurant. He didn't look ten years older to Raja, but he did look sickly. His skin was pale and his eyelids were heavy laden. There were a few gray hairs scattered throughout but if the truth be told, Raja had more. He had simply learned to hide them with hair dye.

Upon seeing Raja, Milton immediately rose to greet him.

"God bless you, my old friend," he extended his arms for a hug, which Raja reluctantly accepted. Such a thing hardly seemed manly, but he could not refuse his long lost friend.

"You too, Jim. You too." Raja seemed at a curious loss for words, so he pulled out a chair and sat down. The two ordered some food, and then stared at one another in silence. The silence was only momentary, but it made it clear that neither was sure what to say. Where to begin? Who would break the ice?

Raja took the initiative. "So where in the Hades have you been?" He chose these words because he did not wish to offend his Missionary friend with expressions of hellfire, but also because he did not wish Milton to believe that he was angry with him. The words, therefore, were harsh enough to show his frustration but light enough to show some humor as well as expressing mild anguish at Milton's long absence.

"I am sorry, Raja. I wish I could have contacted you, but to the outside I world was I dead. I knew that and yet it was impossible for me to abandon my new family."

"Family?" Raja was somewhat taken aback.

"Yes," replied Milton. "I am married to a beautiful Indian woman," he said with a smile.

Raja was now quietly angry. "You mean you have been living in India for all these years and never contacted anyone back here in the states?" His voice was raised, but remarkably he remained rather calm, not wanting Milton to know the extent of his concern or, dare I say, love.

"No no," Milton started to chuckle a little, but his laughter was stifled by a nasty cough. The coughing continued for a brief time and it was apparent that Milton was a very ill man. Upon hearing these brief words, and seeing Milton's physical condition, Raja's quiet anger subsided. Instead, he looked intently upon his old friend for the first time. Milton was pale, and not pale as in

Caucasian, but pale as in deafly. pale. He had no color and his eyes were somewhat red. It was obvious to Raja now that Milton had not had any sleep in sometime. He, therefore, said nothing, but waited for Milton to resume speaking.

"No my friend. I would have contacted you had I been able to, but the truth is, I was trapped. It was a guilded cage to my eyes, but I was still trapped. The Valley had only one entrance and one exit, being the same. I was stuck there; I thought for good."

"Valley?" uttered the curious Raja.

"Yes. A hidden valley. Perhaps the very one we were looking for."

Incredulously Raja exclaimed, without thinking, "you found Shangri La?"

With a smile, Milton simply replied, "Not exactly," and yet there was an ominous tone in his voice, although it may have been his sore throat rather than an intentional tone. In either case, it was clear that the valley they sought existed, but Raja was soon to learn it was no Shangri La. Nor was it Utopia, or any other glorious mythical civilization. Neither was it a dystopian civilization; at least not to its citizens. It was, however, a civilization unlike any in the known world.

Milton continued. "The valley hid a civilization all right, or perhaps a village is a better term. It was not large, nor particularly advanced culture. It was a thousand years old, but there were no monuments to commemorate its founding nor statues to honor its leaders, for they had no use of such things. Even their homes were carved out of the rocks, like caves, with no ornaments or architectural design of note. The reason, you see, is that they were all blind."

"Blind? All of them."

"Yes. They were born blind. Not a single one could see. I had stumbled upon Eramus's mythical 'Country of the Blind.'"

3 – Discovery of the Valley

"Erasmus's mythical 'Country of the Blind.'" These words meant nothing to Raja, but he took a mental note of them nevertheless, for something told him that they were significant.

Desiderius Erasmus was a Renaissance theologian of some note. He prepared a famous Greek text of the Bible from ancient pre-Constantinian copies, he wrote theology and philosophy, and he is claimed by both Catholics and Protestants as one of their own, although in his day both Catholics and Protestants were angered by him. He sought reform within the Catholic Church but rejected Calvinism, despite defending many Protestant doctrines. This much Raja knew. Beyond that Raja was ignorant of Erasmus. After all, Raja prided himself on being a professor of science, not religion or history. He also knew that it was typical of Milton to bring up some obscure long dead theologian in a conversation which, as far as Raja could tell, he had no place. For the time being he put it in the back of his mind, but promised himself to look up the quote in the school library later.

"So tell me what happened," begged Raja.

"Well, you remember when we were scaling the mountain?"

"Of course," said Raja with a slight chuckle.

"Well, I had lost my grip and slipped. I guess you remember that, but I hit my head on a rock and was dazed. At that point it was all hazy but I remember hanging by the cord and looking down beneath me. There was a ledge. A small ledge, but there was a ledge there so I cut the cord and dropped down to the ledge."

"What did you cut the cord for? I was pulling you up!" Raja was bemused and a little frustrated, believing that Milton had better sense.

Anticipating Raja's complaint, Milton replied, "I know, I know, but as I said I was dazed and confused. My head felt like a marsh-mellow. I wasn't thinking clearly at all. In fact, after I dropped to the ledge I lost consciousness."

"So that is why you never replied."

"Yes. I fell unconscious and never heard you. When I came to I was still in a dazed semi-conscious state. To this day I am not sure of what I saw, but I looked up and I saw the shadow of a woman standing at the mouth of a cave."

"Cave? I didn't see any cave on the way up."

"Yes, I know. I am not sure how we missed it, but it was sort of hidden in a little nook. The entrance was not clearly visible. Nevertheless," said Milton, struggling to remember his place, "I struggled to my feet and called out to her, but the shadow was gone. I looked around but there was nothing, and I mean nothing. I had lost my ice pick, my cord, and most of my gear had fallen out of my pack. All I had left was a few days worth of food, and a single canteen of water. Even my extra canteens had fallen off the mountain. I had no chance of scaling down the mountain and making it back.

"I thought about waiting for a rescue plane to spot me, but the air was so thin and I was so cold, I decided to take shelter in the cave. It was pitch dark in there so I could not see clearly, but I heard the sound of water and even animals scurrying in the distance. I began to think that the cave must lead somewhere. Perhaps I wasn't thinking clearly, but I decided to explore the cave."

As Milton told his story, Raja listened intently despite Milton's lack of story-telling ability. The entire story laid out in these next few chapters was told by Milton in but a few short paragraphs. Here then are the details omitted by Milton.

As he entered the cave, it was pitch black, except for the light shining in from the cave entrance. As the sun was setting, even that light faded. Milton was convinced that there was no way back down the steep slopes of ice and he also convinced himself that the figure he had seen was indeed a woman. If a woman had entered into the cave and disappeared then it was apparent that there must be another exit far below in the depths of the cave. This made sense, for the cave was built into a mountain and if there was an entrance near the top of the mountain, there might be an exit near the bottom. Milton knew this because he had studied geology. Caves are usually formed when massive flooding waters carve a hole and seek lower ground. Water always seeks low ground, but how then, one might ask, did water get so high as to carve a cave in a mountainside? As unfantomable as it may seem virtually ever mountain top contain many evidences of flooding. Fossils of fish can be found at the top of mountains, and numerous mountains were even carved by water. The entire desert of the mid-west in America were formed when flood waters carved the Grand Canyon, Carlsbad Caverns, and other testaments to the legends that encompass ancient history. Whether it is the Babylonian legends, the tales of the American Indians, the Chinese, or the Bible, all tell tales of a flood that covered the globe. Even the United States Geological Survey, a government entity, attributed the mid-west desert to flooding which they believed came from melting glaciers in the ice age. Yes, flood waters had carved the beauty of the cave which Milton found himself, though he was unable to see it for he had lost his equipment and had no light.

Milton's first thought was of survival. How was he to crawl down pitch black caves to find the exit? Moreover, how was he too eat and drink? He did not even have a canteen anymore. The solution was more simple that one might think. Snow covered the mountain and the cave provided a perfect drain for melting snow and water. Water could be obtained from the walls, from melting snow, and from little water falls that existed within the caves. As for food, Milton was not fat, but he knew that the human body stored enough food in body fat to allow him to survive for some time. A week without food would be painful, but he would survive. Milton was practical in this regard, and prepared himself mentally for this. He was convinced he could survive a week without food, but he could not survive the bitter freezing cold if he stayed outside the cave. This strengthened his resolve to find another exit.

The greater problem was how he could navigate the caves. His eyes would adjust to the darkness, but eventually even the light from the entrance would be gone as he descended further and further into the cave. The good news is that even the faintest glimmer of light from any exit would be clearly visible and guide his way. It was the interim that frightened Milton. He would have to crawl on all fours, like an animal, being careful to feel his way and to make sure that he did not fall off the edge of any drop. As the cave was very slippery and wet, cave crawling would have to be accompanied by crawling in the most literal sense of the word.

All these things went through Milton's mind. He analyzed his options and choices, for he was a meticulous man. He could not survive the frigid cold of the mountain top waiting for a rescue which might never come. He reasoned that he could survive a week, and that would be time enough to find the exit of the cave, if there was an exit. Although he had no assurance that such an exit existed, he was convinced that the shadowy figure was not his imagination. If another person had been in the cave, then there must be another exit. This reasoning gave Milton a better chance of survival, for he was not one to panic as others might do. He was fully prepared for a week of cave crawling and this gave him his survival edge. Mental preparation was the key to survival.

With his mind set and prepared, Milton began the long descent. For four hours he felt strong and hopeful, but in those four hours he had wasted as much as three of those hours correcting wrong turns which had led to dead ends. Because there was no foot path Milton had to decide where he could crawl down and where he could not. He decided only to take drops that were not steep for there was no way to tell how far a fall might go. There might be a bottomless pit awaiting him. Therefore if he could not plant an arm or leg or foot, he turned back. Occasionally he would drop a rock and listen to hear how long it took to hit a floor. After five hours of this, Milton could still clearly see the entrance but could see no light from below. It was enough to make most men give up. It would not have been hard to return to the top and hope that a rescue party had arrived, but in his heart he knew that Raja had probably not even reached the bottom of the mountain yet. No rescue party would appear for at least another twelve hours, so Milton resolved to continue his quest for at least another six hours.

During this time he took no sleep and refused to close his eyes. His journey seemed to make slow progress as the light was becoming more and more dim from above, but that also meant that Milton was reaching the point of no return. Oddly enough it was a sound that urged him onward. The sound was that of an animal. He could not tell what it was and its sound was like a soft wail. The noise would have made most men turn back immediately, as it sent a shiver up Milton's spine, but Milton was a composed man. In his mind he understood that if there was an animal capable of making such noises deep within the cave, then that had to mean that there *was* another exit. He let out a slight laugh. It was a laugh of joy, for he was now convinced beyond a shadow of a doubt that another exit did exist far down below.

Ten hours had passed. There was no food, but water was not a problem. He easily found pools of water or dripping water from the ceiling. He now forgot completely about going back and moved on forward into the depths of the cave. After three more hours, he had no choice but to take a brief nap. He could not say how long he slept but he was awakened by the sound of bats. What could have scared the bats, he wondered? Perhaps there were more animals in the cave scurrying about. Perhaps he was not far from the exit. Hope filled Milton's heart, renewed by a brief rest. Nevertheless that hope turned to despair for even the best of men find it hard to maintain faith when all seems blackest, and the cave was black indeed. Not even a glimmer of light reflected off the water in the cave; nothing. Milton knew he could not turn back now, but he was scared. Was this to be the end? Was the time God gave him expiring? To each man is given an allotted time and we do not know when that time will end.

These questions raced through his mind as his stomach growled. It was then that a terrible thought crossed his mind. Could it be that the bats heard the rumbling of his stomach? Could that be what disturbed the bats? Milton was no longer thinking rationally. His keen mind was starting to give way to despair for he should have realized that bats do not live where they cannot eat. Consequently, the very fact that there were bats that deep in the cave should have told him that he was closer than he thought.

Milton was on the verge of breaking down mentally and physically when he noticed something he should have noticed hours ago. It was so dark that Milton had grown used to the darkness. His mind visualized the rocks around him, but he could not really see them. Then, like a frog in water, he thought something had changed. If you turn up the heat of a frog slowly it will boil to death without even knowing it, but if you turn up the heat instantly it will notice the heat rise and jump out of the water. In the same way Milton had not even realized that when he was retrieving water he knew where the water was because he could *see* the glimmer of water droplets. Yes, the water was just barely visible, but it *was* visible. It was not his imagination, or was it? He did not think anything about this initially because his mind, tired and exhausted as it was, had visualized the cave around him. It is easy to understand how Milton's mind, in the state it was in, might have been unable to distinguish between dream and reality.

Was he really seeing the water, or just visualizing it? Such a dilemma is common in the psychiatric world. When someone is hypnotized they become unable to distinguish between a dream and a memory; between reality and fantasy. That is why many women dream that they were Cleopatra in a former life, but Cleopatra was only one woman, so no more than one person could be Cleopatra. How then is it that hundreds of women claim to have been Cleopatra in a previous life? Because they *dreamed* it. They did not remember a past life at all, but they dreamed that they were Cleopatra and convinced themselves, with the help of the hypnotism, that it was a "repressed memory." Milton had read about the damage done to people through these "repression therapies" and the number of false "memories" dredged up by quack psychiatrists. Consequently, it took Milton a few moments to grapple in his own mind whether the light was really there or whether he was just hallucinating like a mirage in the desert. Finally, his mind became more clear. He remembered the bats and he remembered that they could not possibly be this deep in the cave unless there was life down there. Either animals or vegetables *must* exist or the bats would not be this deep in the cave. He realized that there was a light at the end of the tunnel and chuckled at the irony of having seen the light for perhaps as much as an hour before he even knew it was there! Such a great irony, but one that is common to the human race.

These events renewed Milton's spirit. He stepped up the pace, but perhaps a little too much. Eager to find the exit, he slipped and slid as much as ten feet before gaining a grip. He could not tell if there was a bottomless pit below, or if he would have just slid another ten feet and hit bottom, but he dared not try. He slowly crawled back up to firm footing and felt around for a better path. He knew he would have to continue to take it slowly. Finally, he came to an edge. The edge was steep; much too steep to climb down, but when he peered over the edge he could now clearly see a glimmer of light. This filled Milton's heart with joy. It was clearly not his imagination, but he began to wonder if it was night or day. The light was faint. It was just a glimmer, but it was light. If it was day then the exit must still be far away but if it was night then the light might be closer. He had lost count of time and had no way of knowing. He briefly said a prayer of thanks and asked for the strength to continue onward.

The closer he got to the exit the more anxious he got, and the more risks he seemed to be taking. He starting moving on two feet rather than crawling on all fours and more than once this lead to near catastrophe. The last time Milton twisted his leg rather severely. He pounded his fist against a rock, which only made him feel worse. He massaged his foot, but he was not able to put any real weight on it. This may have been a blessing in disguise for it forced him to crawl on all fours again and not to push on at too fast a clip. Eventually, he could see the exit clearly. The light was streaming in and it was now obvious that it was daylight outside. He could see the cave and he could see the rocks within it quite clearly. Finally, he stood up and hobbled toward the exit, but as he reached final freedom the light from the sun blinded him. Milton closed his eyes, aware of another irony of nature. He could not see without light but he had been so long without sunlight that he now could not see *because* of the sunlight. The light was shining through his very eyelids and hurt his eyes even with his eyelids shut tight. Thus Milton, finally emerged from the cave, only to fall to his knees again with his eyes closed tight.

Having found freedom, Milton rewarded himself with sleep. No sooner had he fallen to the ground than he fell asleep, sound with the knowledge that he had made it to the bottom of the mountain. Exactly where he was he did not even care. He just wanted to sleep, and that sleep would also give his eyes time to adjust to the light which was still creeping through his thin skin, called by some "eyelids."

Hours passed when Milton was awakened, but it was what awakened him that would change his life. He felt something pushing against him and nudging him. At first he though some animal was punching him. As he opened his eyes, the light still hurt but he could see images. Fortunately, shadows of tall images blocked the direct sunlight and allowed his eyes to slowly focus. He was surrounded by people; many people.

"*Kaun hai*?" said one.

"*Kaun hai*" repeated another.

Milton did not know the language, but assumed it was either Hindi, the main language of India, or perhaps Nepali. He assumed at first that this might be a rescue team that had discovered him, but that illusion was shattered quickly for as his eyes adjusted to the light he saw that these people were all quite different. That is to say they were different from us, but not from each other. They all lacked the same thing.

As Milton attempted to stand, he looked into their eyes and saw only blank white stares. The eyes were white as snow. The pupils were barely visible through a milky white film that covered their entire eyes. Each and every man and woman was blind.

4 – The Valley of the Blind

Milton was in a state of confusion. His mind was in a daze. For a second he wondered if he was in a dream. As he sat up, the small crowd around him was touching his shoulder and back while speaking a foreign language he could not understand.

"*Aapne kya kaha?*"

"*Kya vah mar gaya?*"

"*Vah kaun hai?*"

"*Jiven ko bulao!*"

Finally, Milton stood up with some assistance from two of the men and spoke, saying simply, "does anyone speak English?"

"*Kya?*"

"*Vah kya kah raha hai?*"

The chattering continued and Milton began to wish he had watched more of those Bollywood films his old girlfriend used to watch, but he so hated "chick flicks." He liked the dance numbers packed with beautiful women in bright colorful clothes, but the idealism was too unrealistic for him. The good guys were so pure they made Mother Teresa look selfish and the villains made Hitler look tolerant by comparison. Nevertheless, he had seen enough Bollywood to tell that they were indeed speaking Hindi. In fact, in the years to come his brief stint watching Bollywood films would actually profoundly help his study of the language, for even though he was unconscious of it, he had picked up some Hindi hidden away in the back of his head.

The villagers, although unaware of what Milton was saying, deduced that he was physically very weak. They helped him to a doctor named Jiven who looked Milton over, but the growling from his stomach left no doubt that what Milton needed more than anything was food. To that end a great banquet was prepared on his behalf. There was no table, but a cloth laid out on a grass field. They all sat "American-Indian style" around the banquet cloth, although they were hardly American Indians, but Indians of a different kind. The food was strictly vegetarian, but not disgusting like raw vegetables. They were cooked with Indian spices and something Milton could not recognize. There appeared to be some fruits mixed in creating a rare taste of spice and sweet all at the same time. Their cuisine was obviously descended from India, but over the centuries the cuisine had acquired a taste of its own. The drink was a mixture of oranges, mangos, strawberries, water, and some other fruits that grow only in the valley.

Milton, always a keep observer, watched the people with a keen eye. He observed their customs and nuances. Clearly they had descended from the Indian culture more so than that of Nepal, but they had been separated long enough they had peculiar nuances of their own. How long had they been here? Why were they all blind? Not a single villager could see and yet they had no need of sight. Everything was geared and designed for the blind. The road markers they had set up in place of road signs had different objects hanging on them. Those objects had strong smells. Even Milton, who was not as well trained in the "lower" senses as the people of the valley could smell the distinct odors from a distance.

Each post had a different odor which designated a different area or intersection. The roads themselves were made of different materials. Some had pebbles, some sand, and some used dead grass or hay. Again, the different textures told the population what area they were in and where the road would lead.

All these things told Milton that this village had no contact with the outside world. He did not even have to ask, for it became apparent that they did not even know what sight was. This fact would become more readily apparent, and even ominous in its repercussions.

Across from Milton at the banquet cloth was a beautiful woman. She had no makeup, for what use would the blind have for such things, and her hair was straight with no braids or ornaments such as those designed to tantalize the eyes. Her beauty was natural. It was of the kind made by God rather than man. Although Milton had long learned it was not polite to stare, he found himself doing that just. After all, he reasoned, how would she know he was staring. It wouldn't be rude if she didn't realize it, would it?

Her tan skin reminded him of Hispanic girls back in Texas and her raven hair matched well with her skin. Her face was soft and tender. Her eyes, of course, were milky white. This took some getting used to on Milton's part, for it felt eerie to see those eyes staring off into space, and yet her smile made him forget the eyes. He found himself looking at her lips rather than her eyes whenever he spoke to her.

Forgetting that no one would know to whom he was speaking, he introduced himself to the girl.

"My name is James Milton," he said. It was an elderly man who answered however.

"*Aap ka naam Jams Meelton?*"

Laughing as quietly as possible, Milton replied kindly, "Yes, James *Mil-ton*," he said more slowly and distinctly.

"*Achaa. Mera naam Pita-ji hai. Mujhe log is naam se bulate hai kyuke mai is ghati ka pita hoon.*"

Of course Milton had no idea what he was saying. His Hindi was restricted to the English part of Hinglish. In fact, he still wasn't quite sure what the man's name was. "Pizza-jee Hay?", he guessed.

The elder let out a loud laugh and said, "*Nehi. Mera naam,*" he emphasized these last words, "*Pita-ji,*" then adding, "*hai. Nehi 'Pita-ji hai.' Sirf 'Pita-ji'.*"

"Pita-ji."

"*Vaah! Bahut acchaa. Pita-ji aur,*" the elder, whom Milton had now deduced was named Pita-ji, turned to the beautiful young woman whom had caught his eye, "*ye mere beti Anjali hai.*"

"*Namaste,*" she said.

"Anjali," he said with a smile. "That is a beautiful name, because you are like an angel. I think I will call you Angel-i."

*****

Now it didn't take too many days for Milton to discern why the people of this valley had never met a man with sight before. Although he had escaped the mountain top, he had not escaped the mountains for this valley was surrounded on all sides by sheer cliff faces. The cliffs shot straight up into the air, making it impossible to get out any way other than the way in which he had come. The valley was not a small valley, but it was cut off from civilization. Moreover, the sheer cliffs made the wind swirl around at high altitudes. Consequently, Milton deduced that a helicopter could never get close enough to the valley without being caught up in the winds and crashing. Planes might see the valley, but would fly so far over head that they could not distinguish this valley from any other valley, and there were hundreds of such valleys scattered throughout the vast Himalayas.

Milton didn't dare try to leave too soon. He had barely survived the trip down and if he attempted to leave the way he came he would be faced with many of the same problems. He could gather resources such as food and water, but traveling by himself he figured it would take a month to safely reach the old monastery from whence he and Raja had embarked. He gave a month as the timeline because he figured it had taken almost a week to descend the dark cave. On the way up he could bring a torch, but up is never as easy as down and the path was not marked. Finding the entrance would be harder than finding the exit. Moreover, once he reached the top, he would have to descend again on the outside of the mountain using handmade mountain climbing equipment, for the ones he had bought were no more. Consequently, Milton made up his mind he would not embark for several weeks at least.

Those weeks soon became months and as he learned more and more of these people's languages he was able to speak more and more with Anjali. Soon Milton's heart forgot about civilization as it was concentrating on other things; or at least *one* other thing. He spoke daily with Anjali, learning Hindi and trying to teach her English in exchange. Problems, however, came as he tried to explain sight or used words, so intricately interwoven into our speech, that reflected sight. Simple things like "I see" instead of "I understand" or "look at this" confused Anjali and the others. At first the villagers took this as a language problem. In time, they figured, they would understand each other better, but the months had now become over a year and while Milton's Hindi was far from perfect, it had become increasingly clear to the people that Milton believed he had a *fifth* sense!

Some called Milton crazy. Some saw him as being sent by God. Others called Milton eccentric. Still others suspected him of far worse, but the only ones that counted was Anjali and her father, the Village Elder. Milton would never know how lucky he was that Anjali and Pita-ji trusted him, for there would come a day when Raja would face the same situation, but without Anjali by his side. People are naturally protective, and being sinners, fear can make us do terrible and evil things. Fear stems from the unknown, and to them eyesight was unknown. Just as people fear the occult and its supposed sixth sense, the people of the valley feared this fifth sense, if they believed it at all. This became obvious one day when Milton was walking side by side with Anjali. Now since the Valley had been constructed by and for blind people there were few obstacles for them, but occasionally, for whatever reason, a rock may have slid down from the cliffs and fallen upon a path. As Anjali was walking she did not realize that a large rock lay in her path and Milton naturally warned her. She thought he was joking, but when she tripped over the rock, she became fearful.

"How did you know?" she asked.

He only responded that he could "see" it. Her reaction to this was similar to the reaction we might give if a mystic tells us we will get in a car wreck today, and it happens! She trusted him, but she was afraid. For the first time she realized he really *did* have a fifth sense, and it made her nervous. Things would settle down and return to normalcy, but Milton came to realize that it was better if the people of the Valley did not believe in his sight at all. It is better to be thought an eccentric man than an occult wizard. This was a lesson, however, that Milton would forget to pass on before his untimely death.

The time Milton spent with Anjali passed so quickly that he had purposely forgotten his dream of returning to civilization. He was, after all, a missionary by trade. He had decided that this valley would be his ministry. It was a land untouched by the words of the Jewish Carpenter from Asia Minor. The man who came to redeem all men, whether they be Jewish or gentile. Whether they were pagans who had sacrificed to the gods, devout Jews, or Hindus, Jesus had come that all might turn to the Lord and repent. This "good news" was no longer popular in America anyway. The idea that Jesus was able to save all men was now interpreted by the enemies of religion as the idea that Jesus damned all who disagreed with him. Such was the hatred of the flower children's children. America, founded by Christian doctrines, was now a land where public prayer was challenged and where devout Christians are called terrorist and extremist by Senate leaders. Milton preferred it here. Or perhaps, as the cynic might say, he just preferred being near Anjali.

In either case, this would be his mission. It was a land untouched by the outside world for centuries. How many centuries he did not know, but he had learned from speaking to Pita-ji that they counted time by the generations of their families and by the number of harvests from their fields. He learned that there had been thirty-seven generations since the valley was founded by Pita-ji's ancestor. Further there had been 913 harvest since that time! In short, they had been there almost a thousand years! For this very reason Milton was no longer surprised at the differences with Indian culture, but rather he was shocked that there not more differences.

For example, the religion of the valley was clearly Hindu in tradition, but like the Judeo-Christian faiths they had no idols. This made sense since the people of the valley could not see, why would they need an idol representing a visual depiction of the god? They didn't. For them God could not be represented in a physical form or appearance but in all other respects they remained Hindus. Furthermore, like most Hindus they believed that god dwelled within all men and yet they rejected the notion that God could become a man. This was always an obstacle to many Christians in India, for the average Indian could never accept a man as God incarnate and yet Milton could never quite understand how they could claim every man was an embodiment of god while denying that Jesus could literally be God. In any case, there was a thread of agreement between Milton and the Hindu community there. Since he did not attempt to force his faith upon the people of the valley, for that would be contrary to the teachings of Jesus, he was accepted and never viewed as a threat. Moreover, he discovered that he was not the only one from another religion to have made contact with the valley.

The Buddhist monks had made contact long ago and knew all about the valley. Milton discovered that the monks of the Himalayas, the very ones that had he and Raja had spoken to before scaling the mountain, had long relayed certain information of the outside world and of India to the village, but only a little. They were not messengers but protectors.

The monks had actually intended to send Milton and Raja in the wrong direction. How ironic then that the lack of mountain climbing skills by Milton actually brought them to the wrong peak! Or perhaps it was predestined that Milton would discover the valley. In any case, the monks would eventually come to speak with Pita-ji as they did once every ten harvests. Their next harvest visit was still three harvests away. This gave Milton both hope and an excuse not to try to leave before then. For the next three years he would stay, nurture his new flock, and await their arrival.

Two years had now passed and Milton could speak Hindi quite well. Anjali and Pita-ji, as well as a few others, had learned to speak English in turn. It was in that language that Milton asked for Anjali's hand in marriage. The wedding was performed in the Hindu tradition, with some changes one would expect from a civilization separated from India by a thousand years. She was dressed in a fancy Indian gown, called a "Sari." There were no bright colors upon it, since they had no idea what colors were, but the fabric and style were similar to the wedding dresses of the Punjab in India. Milton likewise wore the traditional Indian clothes fit for a groom, but the colors were white, obviously from the few sheep that lived in the valley. A type of Indian scarf was wrapped upon both Anjali and Milton and then tied to one another, symbolizing that they were "tying the knot" as they used to say in Texas. Of course the tradition existed long before Texas but Milton couldn't help smiling to himself. Marriage was a binding of two souls into one. The tying of a knot was neither eastern nor western. It was a universal symbol of marriage for life.

Next they began to march around a fire and recite vows. Milton wandered how they kept from burning their clothes in the fire, since they could not see it, but he reminded himself that he was thinking as a sighted person, and not a blind person. Could not the blind feel the heat? Their senses were heightened from years of practice so they could probably sense the heat of the flames even more so than Milton. He wanted to slap himself, but then let out a brief giggle. Anjali's head turned back toward him, thinking he was laughing at their marriage, but she knew him too well for that thought to last. She figured it was a laugh of joy, and indeed it was true. Milton the Missionary was getting married.

Now Milton was a Protestant so there was no sin in marriage at all. On the contrary, marriage is sacred. No, the reason this was all so strange to Milton is because he was now almost fifty years of age. He thought that his marriage days had passed him. He had resigned himself to be single the rest of his life, but now not only was he marrying, but he was marrying a beautiful young woman of 28 harvests! After all, she could not see the cracks in his face. She could not see age at all. Years were measured only in harvests, and decades and centuries did not exist; only generations of family. Milton had resolved to spend the rest of his life here with his new family. When the monks came next harvest Milton would not leave with them. He would ask them to take a message back to his friends and surviving family, of which were few, but he would stay here with Anajli the rest of his life. Or so he thought.

*****

It was a cool day when two monks arrived through the cave entrance. A bell rung out and the entire village went to greet the men. Milton accompanied Pita-ji and Anjali but he stood out from the rest. The second the monks looked him in the eye they knew who he was. Oddly, however, they did not speak at once to him. They continued their greetings to Pita-ji and the other council members. At first Milton thought they were being cordial until they adjourned to the council chambers when it seemed apparent that they were deliberately ignoring him. He quietly walked toward the council chamber with Anjali in arm when he looked back and noticed one of the monks gesturing to him. He realized they wished to speak to him in private and had said nothing publicly for that reason.

"I will be with you shortly, Angel-i," he said as he turned back. One of the monks continued on while the other dropped back behind the others and met with Milton.

"So you survived."

"Yes, I found my way here to the valley," replied Milton.

"It is good that they have accepted you."

"It seems you have not accepted me," said Milton coyly.

"Accepted you? Why do you say that?"

"Why did you not speak to me in public?"

"Because we cannot let them know that we can see. How could we acknowledge knowing you from the world outside without acknowledging that we can see? Until they introduce you as one from the outside world we must accept you as a native of this village."

"What?"

"Surely you know by now. They know nothing of sight and distrust those who have it. To them it is like magic."

The monk noticed the expression on Milton's face and realized something he did not dare speak. "How have you survived here? Tell me. Have you never spoken of sight with them before?"

"I tried for a while. There was a language barrier at first so that helped. They thought my words strange, but I am a quiet person by nature and I soon came to see that they would not accept me unless I was one of them. I speak to Anjali of sight, but not to anyone else. Not even to Pita-ji."

"Anjali? The village elder's daughter?"

"Yes. She is my wife."

The monk's eyes lit up and his eye brow raised up high. "Interesting. But we will speak of this later. The council is waiting for us now. My name, in case you don't remember me, is Amran."

This was Milton's first meeting with someone from the outside since he arrived in the valley. The words were not harsh, but something in Milton realized there was a darkness behind them. The monks pretended to be blind and cautioned Milton about speaking of his eye sight. It was no secret that the people of the valley had once considered Milton a bit strange, but the language barrier could literally have saved his life; something he was only now beginning to realize. Eye sight was to them as magic. He had spoken to Anjali of these things, but she had always told him to keep these secrets between themselves. Only now was Milton starting to realize why.

Even more disturbing to Milton were the conversations that followed the next few days. He had asked the monks to take a message back to the world and to his family, but the monks refused. He was told point blank that he was dead to the world and *no one* could ever know the secret of the valley. Milton had already made up his mind to stay in the valley with his family, but he now realized that they would not have taken him out of the valley had he wanted to leave. Thoughts passed through his head so quickly he could not collate them. What if he had not fallen in love with Anjali? What if he had spoken their language from the very start and persisted in speaking about his eyesight? What if he had tried to leave the valley on his own? Would the monks have simply let him leave? Was he a family member ... or a prisoner? He realized now the monks were the protectors of the valley. The valley was their secret and was to be kept at all cost.

5 – The Journey Home

Ten years had passed since Milton arrived in the valley. He had forgotten about the world outside. He knew he could never return there and he had learned never to speak about his sight except on occasion to Anjali. She would sometimes laugh at him. Other times she listened intently. She had come to believe that he had this fifth sense, and that it was a gift from God, but she could never understand it and urged Milton never to speak of it publicly. There were some who saw Milton as gifted. Others saw him as an outsider. He was accepted as family, but never truly accepted as a member of the community.

Despite this Milton was now a part of the village and a part of their society. He had worked for years to translate the Bible into their own Braille language. Of course, it wasn't really Braille, but it was similar in design. It was a written language made up of a series of bumps and dots. One might think of it as a kind of Morse Code which could be felt with the fingers. This was Milton's favorite past time, but of course this was not his career. In the Valley of the Blind there was only one career; culturing and nurturing the food supply. Even Pita-ji worked the fields and helped in the harvest. Still, there was plenty of time for his ministry. Milton was happy. In fact, Milton was happier than he had ever been in the world outside. The valley harkened back to the days of the Biblical Patriarchs when families lived together their whole life. When the families tended their flocks and made their own food and clothes. Outside luxuries were just that; luxuries. They did not have to rely on food supplies from other states or countries. They did not have to work the hustle and bustle of noisy overcrowded cities. They had only each other. Milton was coming to understand these people, and to understand their fear.

Despite Milton's happiness with Anjali and the village, he had become increasingly sad the past year. Anjali and Pita-ji were the only ones who knew why, but it was becoming increasingly clear to the others as well. When he spoke he constantly had a sore throat and spoke with a scratchy voice. This condition was becoming worse as the months passed by. Within the past year everyone had come to realize that Milton was becoming very ill. Jiven had never seen anything like it. The valley doctor was used to many ailments but this was unknown to him. Milton, however, had seen it.

"It is called 'cancer,' doctor."

"Cancer?" replied Jiven.

"Yes, throat cancer" he said with a scratchy voice.

"How do you get this cancer? Where does it come from?"

There was a pause before Milton replied, "I haven't touched a cigarette in ten years, but I supposed I had developed throat cancer back then. These past ten years were a reprieve of sorts. I don't know exactly. The cancer must not have progressed very quickly these past ten years. I have heard that wine can cause throat cancer to progress, but only if used in large quantities. If I was in the early stages of throat cancer from cigarettes before I came here, the wine I have drunk over the past ten years may have slowly caused the disease to progress. Certainly it was not the wine alone, for I have never even been drunk," Milton tried to laugh but found himself unable to.

"I don't understand. What is a cigorat?"

"It is a weed. A plant that we light on fire and smoke. We breath it into our lungs."

"Why?"

With a self mocking laugh, Milton replied, "that is a good question, and one which I cannot answer. Anyway, most people destroy their lungs with cigarettes. That is called lung cancer. Occasionally, you can develop throat cancer, although I am not sure why it took this long after I quit smoking to progress. Maybe the progression had already begun and I was fortunate that it took this long. Maybe it was the occasional wine that aggravated the cancer. Had I still been smoking it would surely have progressed much faster. In any case doctor, there is nothing you can do here."

"Nothing?"

"Not here. Only back in the world I came from do they have a treatment."

Only back in the world from which he came. Word went out throughout the valley. If Milton did not return to his world, he would die. The Village Council met to discuss the matter. They were very confused. Not so much about his return to the world outside as to the cause of this cancer. Why, if smoking causes such problems, do people smoke? Milton explained addiction as best he could, but he didn't really know the answer himself. Humans are a self destructive breed. Even when we know we are killing ourselves, we continue on the path to destruction. This was true of politics, of personal lives, and even of our spiritual life. Whatever is harmful to the human race we seem to thrive upon.

The Council's decision was unanimous. Milton could leave to seek treatment, but the specifics were hotly debated. The monks would not return to the valley for many harvests to come. Milton could not wait. How could he leave on his own? How could he find his way out? The council did not believe in Milton's fifth sense and Milton, perhaps it was an unconscious decision, never brought up the issue, so how could he find his way out without the monks?

"I felt my way down the cave when I came here," he reminded the council, and such was completely true for he had no light to see. "I will proceed upward in the same way. I only ask for a torch to keep me warm and a pick to help me keep my footing."

Of course, the torch was really so that he could see, but the warmth angle was much easier to sell to the council. It was accepted readily. All council members agreed and blessed Milton before his journey.

Milton hugged his wife, who was in tears. Yes, apparently those eyes were still capable of producing tears for blindness does not affect tear ducts. Milton too shed a tear or two promising Anjali that he would return to her within three harvests, perhaps sooner. Of course he did not tell her, but if he returned before three harvests then it meant that the disease had progressed too far. He knew that chemotherapy or whatever treatment he sought would last for several years at least, so he comforted Anjali and assured her that however long he was gone, he *would* return.

Already his voice was scratchy from cancer and this made his promise all the more heartfelt. Anjali finally called out, "let me come!" They had already discussed this so Milton knew that her words more an attempt to convince the council than him, and Milton played along with Anjali. "That is not up to me, *mera saathiya*."

The council members were all silent, as if they knew Anjali's pleas were a cry to them, but they would not bend. Finally, Pita-ji stepped forward, "it is time. Our prayers are with you Milton-ji."

*****

The journey to the top of the mountain cave was even harder than the trip down. Milton was surprised at this since he had a light source this time but there were many dead ends and steep inclines. Going down was only a question of taking it slow enough to insure he did not fall over an edge or into a bottomless pit or trip, but the dead ends were fewer since he could easily jump or slide down paths that were not too steep or far from the ledges below. As the time passed Milton began to ration his food for he realized that the trip would take far longer than expected.

Days passed into a week and Milton lost count of the days soon after. It seemed there were countless dead ends and no clear path on which to take. He knew that if the monks had visited the Valley then there must be a way up and out, but his food rations were quickly running out. When he was finally able to clearly to see snow and light from the cave entrance, he felt as weak as he had when he had reached the cave exit below. It took him no fewer than six hours to reach the entrance even after he had identified it, for the incline was far too steep in many places.

Milton's joy upon reaching the entrance quickly met the harsh reality of the biting cold wind slapping his face and a quick glance down the sheer cliffs of the mountains. He had lost any real mountain climbing equipment and now recognized that scaling down the mountain without any real gear would probably take as long as crawling down the cave, but within the cave he was at least protected from the biting cold. There was no such luck here.

After this, everything became hazy in Milton's memory. He only remembered falling unconscious and awakening in the monastery nearby. The monks had found him and taken him in. Inside one of his pockets they also discovered a letter written in a kind of Braille. It was a letter from the Council to the guardian monks granting him permission to leave. Milton had finally made it out of the Valley; the only one to ever leave the valley alive.

6 – The One-Eye Man is King

Raja looked into Milton's eyes with amazement and a little sadness. He wanted to blurt something out of his mouth, but remained remarkably under control, wisely choosing sympathy over exuberation.

"So have you seen the doctor? What did he say?"

Milton coughed, almost as if on cue, and with a scratchy voice, replied, "I am afraid it is too late, my friend." There was a sense of acceptance in his voice. All Milton had ever wanted in life was to make a difference in people's lives, and he felt like he had, at long last, achieved that in his adopted home.

Raja was suspicious of such acceptance of death. To him it was nothing more than resignation. He looked upon such attitudes in the same light as suicide, though curiously enough he had always been a staunch defender of the "right to die." This irony can only be explained by Raja's utilitarian view of life. A man who does not want to live is of no use to the world or society. He did not believe in a heaven or a hell, so there was no eternal fate at stake and no sanctity of human life. He *respected* life, mind you, but he had no sympathy for those who do not want to live. To Raja it was about respect, not sanctity.

"I am sorry, Jim." He paused, not knowing what to say. Death was one thing Raja could never really relate to, seeing as how he had never died. Finally, he said, "What do you plan to do?"

"I am going back to the Valley to live out my last days with my beloved wife."

"Take me with you!" Raja blurted out these words without even thinking. He regretted them almost as soon as he said them, but not because of the words so much as the insensitivity.

Milton shook his head. "No Raja. I do not think that is a good idea."

"But why? We went out on an expedition to find this valley and now we have."

Milton ignored the "we" comment and calmly replied, "I do not want to exploit these people."

"Exploit? Why do you say that?"

"They are a valley of blind people. What do you think would happen if the outside world knew about the valley? Their very way of life could be destroyed by interlopers with suspect motives. Probably the first thing that would happen would be to have a cadre of filmmakers descending upon them to make a reality TV show."

Raja shook off the idea of a reality TV show, although in the back of his mind he thought that sounded like a great idea. Instead, he pretended to be slightly offended, "I am not going to exploit these people. This is a great discovery. Think how it can contribute to our understanding of civilization and evolution."

No sooner had Raja said it than he realized his mistake. Milton smirked a bit and replied, "There is that old inductive logic again, working overtime."

"Inductive logic?"

"Yes, I prefer deductive logic like Isaac Newton and Sherlock Holmes. Examine the evidence and then 'eliminate the impossible and whatever is left, however unlikely *must* be the truth.' That is deductive logic. It is what leads to the inevitable reality of God. Nature is neither eternal nor self creating, ergo its creation *must* be supernatural."

"Oh boy, here we go again," thought Raja. He was about to argue about the so-called "'god' particle" but he knew that scientists had not really found such a thing. They discovered a new subatomic particle in which mass is transferred from something called a "Higgs field"; that is all. It does *not create* mass. The American media is notoriously gullible when it comes to science, and Milton always reminded Raja of the infamous "discovery of cold fusion" back in the 1980s. Cold fusion would eliminate all the negative aspects of nuclear energy and allow people to keep nuclear generators out in their back yards. The energy problems of the world would be solved. The only problem. It didn't really happen and the media *never* retracted their hyped up news reports. Literally countless other examples of media misreporting on scientific "discoveries" could be cited, so Raja decided he would wait until this "'god' particle" (a term the atheists actually hate) was truly discovered, and he was *sure* it would be someday. After all, how *else* could the universe have come into being? Therefore, Raja instead said, "and what does this have to do with inductive logic?"

"Inductive logic is used to 'test' theories by seeing whether or not the evidence *can* fit the theory. You *begin* with an assumption and then see if the evidence fits it. That is fine except that it is only useful to a degree. Evidence can often fit multiple theories. For example, it is absurd to claim that 'red shifts' are proof of a 'Big Bang' when the 'red shifts' are also consistent with entropy as supported by Creationists. Consequently, 'red shifts' supports both theories and cannot be used as evidence of one over the other. That would be disingenuous, and yet this sort of inductive reasoning is constantly used as 'proof' of one view over another by people such as yourself."

All of this was already giving Raja a headache. He did not want to get into another debate about science and religion with Milton, particularly since Raja always seemed to loose those arguments. He therefore resorted to the old change of topic scheme, reliable as ever, "I though missionaries wanted to help people like this?"

"I am."

Raja paused for a second, realizing that he was antagonizing Milton more than convincing him. "Can you make it back alone?"

Milton's expression was hard to gauge, but Raja knew he was on the right path. "Look, I will just document everything. I won't reveal the location of the valley to anyone. I will help you to get back there and keep a record of everything which happens. You know you need my help. You almost didn't make it out. How will you make it back alone?"

Milton looked at Raja with a squint and made sure there was a dramatic pause before he spoke. In this way, Raja would not think he was going to win so easily, but in reality Milton had already determined he would let Raja go. He just wasn't going to let Raja know that he had already made up his mind.

"If you come, you realize that it may be impossible for you to get back alone. These people will not help you to leave unless they trust you completely."

"Then I will earn their trust, just the way you did," Raja said confidently.

Shaking his head, "I don't think it is a good idea, my friend."

"At least think about it. You have a marvelous discovery and a great chance to make a difference with these people. You will need someone to take back your writings and discoveries, right? Don't you trust me?"

Milton smiled, but said nothing.

"You know you need me," retorted Raja.

Again Milton said nothing, instead coughing and drinking some water.

"Well, I am at least going as far as Lucknow with you. Okay? We can discuss the rest when we get there." Raja knew now that Milton was going to let him go, so he smiled broadly, but this was greeted with more ominous silence by Milton, who finally spoke somberly.

"We will discuss this tomorrow. I am tired, and in case you forgot" Milton got up to leave, but turned back to Raja with a soft glare, "I am dying."

The words struck Raja's conscious. He had never known how to deal with death and he realized that he was being insensitive. It was not intentional, but how can a man who believes in neither heaven nor hell dare to look death in the face. For Raja it an eternity of non-existence. Like so many in history, he believed this was his only life and his only existence. He wanted to get as much out of this life as he could before he died, and he did not worry about the afterlife. Milton used to say that this bread amorality, for the one who fears no God, and strives for his own happiness cannot make others happy and does not think of the moral consequences of his actions. Raja always resented that. He was not pure, to be sure, but he did not think of himself as immoral or bad. Raja always thought of himself as a good man.

Raja stood up and hugged Milton. They did not say another word and departed. Milton went up to his hotel room, but Raja headed somewhere else. He headed to the library. There was something about this whole conversation that made him eager to read more about this Desiderius Erasmus.

*****

The library was a bit rustic, but the school liked that look. It made it appear more learned somehow and yet there is an irony of looking at books covered in dust while claiming to be learned. Even more ironic was the first verse Raja read as he opened the pages of Desiderius Erasmus' Collected Works. It read:

> "I consider as lovers of books not those who keep their books hidden in their store-chests and never handle them, but those who, by nightly as well as daily use thumb them, batter them, wear them out, who fill out all the margins with annotations of many kinds, and who prefer the marks of a fault they have erased to a neat copy full of faults."

Such were the words of Erasmus, famed Reformation age theologian, philosopher, and scholar. As Raja thumbed through the book, he found many such quotations.

> "Do not be guilty of possessing a library of learned books while lacking learning yourself."

> "You must acquire the best knowledge first, and without delay; it is the height of madness to learn what you will later have to unlearn."

Raja thumbed through again;

> "It is an unscrupulous intellect that does not pay to antiquity its due reverence."

To this, Raja thought, "dribble." He thumbed through some more;

> "It's the generally accepted privilege of theologians to stretch the heavens, that is the Scriptures, like tanners with a hide."

This one brought a smile to Raja's face. Still he thumbed through some more. Finally, he saw the reference. This particular edition had multiple translations from the Latin. "In the kingdom of the blind, the squinter rules," but the better translation was:

> *"In the country of the blind, the one-eyed man is king."*

7 – The Guardians of the Valley

India is the second most populous country in the world containing almost 20% of the earth's population and yet possessing only around 2% of the earth's land mass. Despite this there are great vacant, empty, and open spaces where people could live, grow food, and expand. India is not overpopulated but underdeveloped. The big cities are overpopulated to be sure, for the poor flock to the big cities looking for something they cannot find elsewhere. India's resources are plentiful but like many countries, they are untapped. The large metropolitan areas rely on resources made elsewhere, so that no one actually makes his own. This is the fundamental problem; it is not overpopulation as the dictator likes to say, but underdevelopment. The solution is not population control but better use and development of resources and the expansion of suburbs, rather than urban development.

Raja and Milton arrived in Lucknow late in the afternoon. Lucknow itself is the capital city of the state of Uttar Pradesh in India, and borders Nepal. It is a city of four and a half million people from various backgrounds. Contrary to western assumptions, Indians come in all different colors, complexions, and heritage. Uttar Pradesh is made up of Indian castes and groups ranging from Bengalis to Punjabis and Anglo-Indians. Approximately 70% of Lucknow is Hindu. The largest minority group are the Muslims who represent just over a quarter of the populous. Sikhs, Jains, Christians, and Buddhists comprise the remaining 4 to 5%. The city is also fairly well educated as nearly 70% of the people are able to read and write.

Amran, the monk from the monastery, met Milton at the airport. This was not that unusual as monks were not so completely cut off from civilization as assumed in the west. They preferred the solitude of the mountains so they could concentrate on learning and prayer, but visits to the cities were not at all uncommon and Amran was usually the one who left. He had received notice of Milton's return, and learned that someone would be returning with him. This was something which did not sit well with Amran or the other guardians of the valleys. Nevertheless, Milton promised to explain when he arrived.

They entered a large luxury hotel. It was not the sort of hotel that Amran, or even Milton, were used to but the University was footing the bill for this trip as Raja had convinced the board this was a historical discovery. Of course, Milton immediately inquired how it could be such a momentous discovery if they were going to keep it a secret, to which Raja replied that only the location would be kept secret, but the discovery would be documented. For some reason Milton neither responded nor argued.

The lobby of the hotel was unlike anything the general public were used to. The typical three star hotel in India is equivalent to a two star hotel in the United States, but this must have been a six star hotel, for its decor rivaled even the best hotels back in the states and the ball room was even more splendid. Both Raja and Milton sat down in the ballroom and awaited Amran who was taking care of accommodations. The were served food called *pakodas*, but is pronounced pako*r*as. This is because the Hindi alphabet, which is technically the Devanagari alphabet, has three letters which correspond closely to our D and R. The letter used here is like when we "roll our Rs." The tongue hits the roof of our mouth as it does with a D. Consequently, the letter D is used to transliterate this letter, even though it often creates confusion for the English speaker. *Pakodas* themselves are a kind of fried vegetable with Indian spices. It is often considered a snack food in India.

While they waited for Amran they saw a dance performance straight out of a Bollywood film, and literally so. In India, Bollywood music sometimes earns more than the movie. Bollywood song writers are almost as big of stars as the actors (called "heroes" in India) and the Indian public even know the names of all the playback singers who remain largely anonymous in American films. The performance was filled with glitz and glamour, not to mention beautiful women wearing clothes they would not be allowed to wear in the public streets. Nevertheless, even this "decadence" was tame compared to America.

The song was, of course, in Hindi, the official language of India. In fact, there are countless languages in India as its various caste and villages and states still remain to a large extent independent of one another. Some villages remain as they were hundreds of years ago with little contact from the metropolitan world. The language of Hindi takes its name from the country and people. Hindi is the language. Hindu is the dominant religion. Hindustan is the country, which is abbreviated to Hindia, or simply India in English. All these words stem from the root word *Hind* (हिंद).

When the song had finished, Amran was just entering the ballroom, looking for Milton. He came over and sat down. Amran had already gone over the amenities when they came to the hotel, so he started straight out on business.

"As you know, the wind conditions make it impossible to get a helicopter into that valley and there is no place to land a small plane. The entrance is through the cave you have already passed through. You will need supplies for a week and we will provide a map so you can find your way more easily. I will take you as far as the monastery, but from there you will proceed on your own."

"Yes," replied Milton, "*danyavad.*" Turning to Raja, he continued. "That is the same monastery we were at before, and the one that found me when I was unconscious after returning from the cave."

Raja grumbled. "The one that lied to us before?"

Amran replied on behalf of Milton, being slightly offended. "Did we lie? We warned you of the dangers and pointed you in the right direction or Jim would never have found that cave at all."

Raja felt that was a half-truth at best, but said nothing as he did not wish to antagonize Amran. Had he wished to speak, however, he would not have been heard for Milton immediately began coughing, and not just a mild cough, but the kind which brought blood. He used his napkin to disguise the cough and hide the blood, but Raja could see a trickle of blood from his mouth as he wiped it. Both Amran and Raja were somewhat speechless as it was becoming more and more apparent that Milton had hid the severity of his condition. The disease had progressed too far for therapy to do anything but prolong the inevitable. His decision to return to Anjali was clear. He wanted to die with his family, but Raja and Amran secretly wondered if he would get that chance.

After a sympathetic pause, Raja spoke out. "Jim, you know you need my help. You are in bad shape. What if something happens on the way? You need me to help or to get help." He paused again, finally saying in a softer voice, "You need my help, friend."

Milton said nothing, but to everyone's surprise, it was Amran who spoke up, "He is right. You can't do it alone."

"You know you need me."

Without missing a beat, Milton answered, as if he has rehearsed the answer before hand. "And you know that you will not be able to return from the valley for years ... if ever."

His emphasis upon those last two words was deliberate and Raja knew it, but he answered bravely saying, "You returned. I will return someday as well, but not until I have recorded everything we see there. Think about it. Think how this can tell us how to better serve and teach the blind here. Not for me, for the people that can be helped, Jim."

To this Milton let out a strange smile, as if he knew something no one else knew. "I wouldn't have let you come this far if I wasn't thinking of letting you come, Raja, but we know each other very well, and I will try with all my heart to talk you out of this."

Raja was at first offended by the implication of "we know each other very well," but he couldn't help but smile himself.

"Remember Raja. These are my family. They are my people. I want what is best for them."

"Yes, of course."

"And one more thing," there was an ominous, and deliberate, pause at this point.

"Yes?"

"They will not trust you just because you are my friend. You must earn their trust."

"I will as you did."

Amran, sensing some mild tension, intervened with joyous voice as if oblivious to the tension. "Great! It is settled. We leave for the monastery tomorrow."

Milton, Raja, and Amran all exchanged handshakes and even a hug or two before heading off to their rooms. There was much to think about, and they needed much rest. The airplane had not allowed them to sleep much and jet lag was already hitting them hard. Although it was only sundown, they planned to sleep until dawn, but it was a plan which Raja could not execute for he spent most of the restless night thinking, and remembering. Their last expedition seemed like a dream to him now. He couldn't help thinking to himself, "Why?" "Why did Milton not answer me?" "What really happened?"

It was not as if Raja did not believe Milton, but such thoughts are natural for anyone. For the past ten years Raja had lived with the horrifying thought that he had killed Milton. Not intentionally of course, but he had pushed an inexperienced mountain climber to scale one of the greatest mountain ranges in the world. He would never admit it, but he blamed himself for Milton's apparent death. He had even used Milton's presumed death as an excuse to embitter his soul against religion. After all, thought Raja, they would never have scaled that mountain at all if they had not been searching for some religious utopian myth.

Such thoughts were not rational, and therefore never came to the surface. Even Raja was not fully conscious of these thoughts. This is human nature. Under the surface we have many thoughts which are not rational. Even the most scientifically inclined are often governed by emotion. Their intellect becomes a front and a defense. The "facts" are not facts at all, but interpretation of selective facts. Truth is supplanted by enlightened opinions. This was the struggle of Raja's mind his whole life, but until he recognized this, he would continue to hide behind his subjective views of selective facts. It was these "facts" that kept him awake most of the night.

At six A.M. came his wake up call. He had scarcely three hours of sleep, on and off, but he knew he could not sleep until he saw this valley. Never had Raja been so intrigued. It was not just a valley of blind men and women, but a new civilization. He imagined himself like a new Columbus, or perhaps a new Cortez. Which one he had not decided, but the quote from Erasmus continued to run through his head.

There was a small town about 90 miles from the monastery. They arrived at the town by taxi around one in the afternoon as the traffic kept them from leaving Lucknow for hours. They made good time after escaping the crowded city, but the roads were not built for race cars, so they could not push the car more than 40 miles per hour most of the trip. Amran suggested everyone take a break and grab a big lunch, for they would not reach the monastery until late in the evening. The taxi would take them to the base of the mountain, but from there they would have to walk on foot.

Milton's health slowed the climb somewhat as he found it harder to breath. His cancer also made inhaling through his mouth somewhat painful at times, and he had frequent needs of rest. It was becoming increasingly clear that Milton was not going to live long. Raja and Amran alternated helping Milton when the occasion needed, but it also made it apparent that someone would have to escort Milton down to the valley. He simply could not make it on his own. Raja was no longer worried about being left behind. Instead, he was worried about being left alone.

It was about an hour before sundown when they reached the monastery. Considering everything, they had made good time. The monastery itself was beautifully decorated. Raja did not recognize much of the art or symbols, but a swastika featured prominently about the archway. This did not surprise Raja, but it had always ignited his curiosity. He knew that the swastika was seen in the west as a symbol of

Nazism, but most had no idea of what Nazism was or what it stood for. Many were even ignorant of the fact that it was the National Socialist Party. They had been so used to the media in the west portraying Nazis as "right wingers" that they were oblivious to its socialist roots. They were also oblivious to the fact that Hitler was a mystic. This is why he borrowed the swastika from eastern religions. Hitler not only hated Jews, but also the evangelical Christians who worship a Jew. Evangelicals were expelled from Germany and the liberal churches (which denied the deity of Christ) were compelled by law to teach that Hitler was the reincarnation of Christ. Of course Christians do not believe in reincarnation at all. The Biblical book of Hebrews teaches that "it was appointed for man to die once, and then comes judgment." Consequently, Christians were among the most persecuted groups of Germany after the Jews who felt the brunt of Hitler's wrath.

None of this had anything to do with Buddhism or Hinduism, save that they shared a belief in mysticism and reincarnation. The swastika, therefore, had no sinister connotations, but it always proved the topic of discussion with his students whenever Raja brought back pictures of a monastery.

The wind was biting so Amran, Milton, and Raja all entered the monastery as quickly as they could without appearing to intrude. The customary courtesies were observed, and the monks gestured for them to enter. So eager was the ailing Milton to get in from the cold that he bumped Amran accidentally, pausing for a second to apologize, but barely loosing stride. Of course the monastery was just that; a monastery. It was not a hotel and had no central heating. The walls prevented too much cold from entering or too much heat from escaping, but the only source of heat were their bodies and a few small oil lamps, used for lighting and incense; not heat. The smell of incense filled the room.

Milton laid down on a cot to rest. Raja sat next to him, and Amran kneeled on a cot to their left. Two monks left, while a third moved one of the candles from a reading table and set it down next to Milton.

Finally, the monk, whose name remained unknown to both Milton and Raja, spoke. "So you have returned. Did the doctors treat you?" His tone was neither brash, nor sensitive, and Raja watched him carefully, pondering his motives. Raja had not forgotten what he would insist until his dying day was a deception by them all those years ago. He did not remember this monk, but he didn't care. They were all the same to him.

Milton replied in a scratchy voice, "Yes, but unfortunately the cancer has progressed too far." He paused secondarily, but resumed before anyone could express condolences, "I could have stayed and undergone extensive treatment, but it would only delay the inevitable."

"Our prayers are with you," replied the monk, but Milton continued as if he never even heard the reply.

"I have chosen to die with my wife in the Valley."

The monk nodded, and Amran placed his hand upon Milton's shoulder, but said nothing. Raja nodded his head in respect, but didn't know what else to say or do.

There was brief silence, when a second monk, who had entered unnoticed spoke, *"Kitne logo ko aap ne is ghati ke baare me bataya hai?"* This was Hindi, for "How many people have you told about the Valley?"

Now while Raja was Indian, he had left India as a child and been raised in America so he never bothered learning Hindi, only Tamil, the language of many south Indians. He suspected the monks knew that, and grew irritated at their speaking in a "foreign" language. His irritation grew when he saw that Milton replied in Hindi.

"Bas apne karibi dosto ko. Kisi ko is jagh ke baare me nahi pata aur waise bhi koi vishwas nahi karega." Milton's Hindi was near perfect. Having lived in the Valley for ten years, they taught each other their respective languages, but Hindi was the language they most often spoke, so Milton had learned it well. This meant, "Just my closest friends. No one knows the location, and no one would believe them anyway."

The monk glanced at Raja quickly, and said, *"Kya aap is aadmi ko ghati me le kar ja rahe hai?"* meaning "Is this man going with you to the Valley?"

"Ji haan. Yes."

"Kya aap ko yakeen hai ke aap is aadmi per viswas kar sakte hai?" meaning simply, "can you trust him?"

"Mujhe uske jarurat hai," meaning, "I need him."

The rest of the conversation I shall translate, for the monk then replied in Hindi, "You know we have been the Protectors of the Valley for nearly a thousand years now. Although we trust you, we cannot allow our friendship for you to jeopardize the safety and secrecy of the valley."

"I understand, but once he enters, there is but one exit. You guard that exit, so there is nothing to fear."

"You mean he will never return to his home?" the monk glanced over at Raja who was staring intently at the men as if he could understand every word they said, and he could, of course, understand none of it.

There was a pause, and some thought before Milton's reply. It was calmly said, "I don't know, but I do know this. If he cannot be trusted then he will never leave the valley. My people know how to protect themselves."

The solemn reply was just this; "Yes. I fear they can."

The monk then bowed his head, even turning to Raja and giving the same respect. He then left the room without a word.

Raja was more than a little irritated, for he knew that he was the subject of the conversation. Whatever could be said of Raja, he was no fool.

"Well, are you going to tell me what he said?"

Milton tried in vain to lighten the mood. "You are Indian. I am White American. How is you can't understand them but I can." He let out a chuckle, but met only Raja's calm stare. It was not an angry stare, for Raja knew Milton was trying to spare him, and yet

Raja wanted his expression to betray his desire. After a short moment of embarrassment for a poor joke poorly told, Milton replied, "He asked if I can trust you."

"And what did you reply?"

At this Milton broke out in laughter and slapped Raja on the back. Without stopping Milton left the monastery still laughing. Despite this, and even because of it, Raja let out a small smile, and turned to followed Milton.

He found Milton standing by a cliff looking down at the beautiful mountains. There was a peace in that place, far from the hustle and bustle of the big cities. The only sound to be heard was the whistling of the wind, and the scenery glistened with moonlight. They stood there together for a moment, saying nothing when Raja broke the silence.

"Why don't you trust me, Jim?"

Slightly offended, Milton answered, "It is not that I don't trust you. It is that I fear for you."

"Fear?" he unconsciously let out a brief laugh, "What is there to be afraid of?"

Milton pressed his lips together. It was not the cold, but his thoughts that was the cause. He wanted to spare Raja's feelings, but he also was torn as to whether or not Raja should come at all. Was it selfish of Milton to take Raja with him? There was certainly something Milton knew about the valley and its residents that Raja did not, and that made a foreboding thought. It was for this very reason that Milton seemed to be trying to push Raja away. He wanted him to come, but he didn't want to take responsibility for what he knew, in the back of his head, would happen.

"I don't believe you will fit in. I don't think you will ever truly be a part of my people. And I fear they will never let you leave."

Many thoughts raced through Raja's head. What did he mean by "my people?" How would they stop him from leaving? What was there to fear in a small village of blind men and women? He looked off in the horizon and surveyed the Himalayas. Milton walked back toward the monastery to leave Raja in his thoughts, but Raja was stubborn, and he knew it. Somehow the forbidden becomes all the more desirable. He wanted to know what the secret of this valley might be. He wanted to know why it was guarded. Most of all, he wanted to know if it was true that "in the valley of the blind, the one-eyed man was king."

Finally, Raja mustered his thoughts, and turned back toward the monastery. He saw Milton and Amran talking to one another and as he approached they turned to greet him.

"If you change your mind tomorrow, you will have my blessing. This is not a path you have to choose," said Milton.

To this Amran added with a laugh, "And I will take you back to Lucknow and introduce you to that girl I saw you eyeing at the hotel."

To add to this mystery, Raja felt more mystery was the best option, so he said nothing. Let them wonder what he was thinking. Let them believe that he had not already decided, but on the morrow he would go with Raja to the valley. Nothing could make him turn back. The secret of the valley was waiting to be discovered.

As they lay down on the cots, Milton had already fallen fast asleep, but Raja could not. It wasn't just the excitement of what lay ahead; it was the bumpy uncomfortable cots that made it impossible for him to get any sleep. He lay restless for a while, when he decided to pull the copy of Erasmus out of his backpack. Perhaps reading could help him get to sleep, he thought.

Now Amran was a light sleeper. He could hear Raja fidgeting around. Finally, he looked over to see what he was doing and spoke quietly, so as not to wake Milton.

"What is that?"

"Erasmus."

"Erasmus?"

"Erasmus." Raja found a stopping point and continued, "He was a famous Renaissance theologian. He was renowned for compiling a copy of the Bible based on the pre-Constantinian Greek texts. He was also a theologian and philosopher; sometimes claimed by both Protestants and Catholics as one of their own."

"Oh, I see. You are a missionary like James?"

Raja laughed as quietly as possible out of deference to Milton, and replied, "Not in a thousand years. I am more of an agnostic. What intrigues me about Erasmus is a saying of his."

"Saying? What saying is that?"

"In the Valley of the Blind the one-eyed man is king."

Amran eyed Raja suspiciously, but decided to play coy. "What does that mean?"

"Well, of course, it was allegorical when he said it. A blind people are easy to rule, but here is a whole civilization that is literally blind. Think about it."

"Yes, what about it?"

Smiling to himself, "Think how a man with eyesight could change them? Think of all I could do for them? Think of it." Under his breath, Amran thought Raja's final words were, "I could be their savior."

"Too many 'I's for my taste," he replied. Pausing, not sure if Raja had intended to be heard, Amran added "besides, your friend would say that they already have a savior."

Somewhat embarrassed, Raja stammered but said, "Who? Him?"

"Jesus of Nazareth, the Jewish carpenter from Asia Minor."

"Oh him," laughing to himself again, "I don't believe in him."

With a note of dissatisfaction Amran uttered "I know" in a low disapproving tone.

Taken somewhat aback, Raja, already quick to talk to slow to think, said, "What? Are you a Christian? I figured you were Hindu."

Amran now spoke in a stern, but not angry, voice. It sounded much as Raja's father when he lectured him as a small boy, and it was the tone that caught Raja's attention. Amran said, "Actually we are Buddhist here, but I know James, and I have known many missionaries. They are often accused of wanting to rob our culture and way of life. Fear has even led many here in India and Nepal to persecute Christians, and particularly missionaries, but I do not believe that their intentions are evil. The insecure fear differences. Fear drives men to extreme actions but those who are secure in their beliefs do not fear. Will not truth prevail? If a missionary lies, will not time prove his work useless? If he speaks the truth, will not time reveal the fruit of his labor?"

"You are a philosopher."

Amran was not yet through with his lecture, "I am also a realist. God and time have a way of revealing the truth of all things. What your friend built will last. What you build may crumble before your very eyes. Be careful what you build, because you will have to live in that house and whether it stands or falls, and it will stand or fall with you in it."

Raja was slightly irritated by all this. He had only said that he could help a valley of blind men and his motives were being questioned without reason or cause. He tried not to let his anger show, but closed the book and placed it back into his pack. He then laid back, saying only, "Good night philosopher."

The reply was this, "Only time will tell."

*****

The next morning they set out to find the cave entrance. Milton was having much more trouble breathing as his cancer made it particularly hard to breath under any circumstances, but the thin air made things even more difficult. They stopped many times upon the way to help Milton catch his breath.

Finally, after three and a half hours, Raja, Milton, and Amran reached a small ledge. Raja recognized the view, but not the ledge. Milton, on the other hand, looked like a dog sniffing for a bone. He rushed off to a small corner and began digging in the snow as if searching for a lost bone. Raja just looked on in amazement.

"Yes, yes!" Milton exclaimed, "This is it."

After digging some more he found a little flag. It was a marker that he had placed there when he had left the cave. He then looked for a large boulder near the ledge.

"Yes. There it is. We must go that way." Milton was so excited that he could hardly breath at all, but there seemed no stopping him. He was more anxious than anyone to return to what was now his home, and his illness made it all the more urgent. This urgency was so apparent that Raja and Amran often exchanged glances without saying a word. They knew that Milton had not long to live and that he only wanted to return to his family before dying.

After scaling up two small rock ledges, Milton shouted down excitedly. "This is it! This is the entrance."

Raja and Amran followed, but Amran was curiously quiet, as if he had known the entrance to the cave all along.

"This does look familiar. No wonder we missed it the first time," pondered Raja.

The ledge they were on was very narrow and not even. It jutted out at about a twenty degree slope. He looked up and examined the surroundings. Although ten years had passed, the memories of that day were etched in his mind. "That is where you fell from! It is a miracle you even managed to land on this ledge instead of tumbling down further!"

"Yes, miracles happen every day, my friend."

Raja felt another theological lecture coming on, so he was careful in his response, "Yes. Maybe. Maybe."

Amran now spoke for the first time since they reached the cave entrance. His words were harmless, but Raja did not like him, did not trust him, and the words made him angry, but they implied something Raja always suspected: Amran knew where the entrance to the cave was all along.

"I am afraid I must leave you now. I will trust you," he said turning to Raja, "to take care of James. He has become a part of us, and we are the guardians of the Valley. If you return, we will be here to help."

With these words Amran turned around and began to scale back down the mountain. Raja was furious, but tried to hide it for Milton's sake. He admitted being a guardian, which meant he knew where the valley lay, but what really infuriated Raja was the simple words, "*if* you return." They wreaked of a threat, but Raja did not distinguish between a threat and a warning, for like most people, his pride made the two equal.

He stood staring down the mountain as if in a trance when James, in a scratchy voice, spoke. "Come, my friend. I am anxious to return, and the trip down to the valley will take many days."

8 – Journey Through the Caverns

One might do well to wonder how a cave labyrinth from high upon a mountain could lead down to an exit near the bottom of a mountain. Unfortunately, there are great misconceptions about cave formations and caverns.

Most caves are formed by water, and water can actually be one of the most destructive forces on earth. Hurricanes can devastate entire cities by the force of wind and water. So powerful are water currents that the vast majority of rocks on this earth are actually sedimentary rocks which were formed by water. The sheer power and force of water pressure bakes, so to speak, mud and dirt and other elements together to create sedimentary rocks. When animals become trapped in these rocks they become fossilized. Fossils are, therefore, formed almost instantaneously when a flood event of a massive scale traps and entombs the poor creature.

Now another misconception can be remedied by revelation of the fact that the entire mid-western desert of the United States of America was formed by vast flood waters. The Grand Canyon was not formed, as sometimes said, by millions of years of gentle rainfall. If this were so then should not the entire earth be a grand canyon? Are we to believe that gentle rain water from New York rolls across hundreds of miles down to the Arizona desert to carve a canyon? Of course not! Rain water soaks into the earth until it evaporates and goes back into the sky. However, if there is too much water for the ground to hold, then the water will dig a trench and seek lower ground. This forms creeks. Only when there is too much water for the creek to hold will it then dig deeper. The rain water does not dig until it has nowhere else to go. Consequently, if a canyon is a hundred meters deep it will never grow deeper unless there is a hundred and one meters of water. It will then remain a hundred and one meters deep until there comes a flood of a hundred and two meters or more.

It follows that the Grand Canyon, in the middle of the great Arizona desert, was once filled to the brim with water! This has been acknowledged by the U.S. Geological Survey which believes that flooding from melting glaciers in antiquity formed the entire mid-western desert of the United States. However, do not expect that you will hear this fact if visiting the Grand Canyon, because the agnostics, like Raja Sinha, do not wish to admit this. "Why" is a curious tale, and one which must be told.

Agnostics, and particularly atheists, are an insecure breed. They claim that religion is the cause of infinite wars, and wars have indeed been fought many times over religion, but it was atheists like Stalin, Mao Tse-Tung, and Pol Pot who butchered more people than all the religions of human history combined. Oddly this is because, in part, they are intimidated by religion. Even though more historical evidence exist, both religious and secular, of the life and times of Jesus Christ than of Julius Caesar, many an atheist, having spent too much time on the internet, try to even deny that such a man as Jesus ever existed! References by pagan historians are rejected or accused of being fraudulent additions with no evidence to support the accusation. This is because they fear that if they acknowledge one single aspect of truth in Jesus, they must acknowledge it all. This is the strength of Jesus, for His life, death, and resurrection cannot be taken separately. They stand or fall together. Consequently, the atheist fears to acknowledge even the most basic historical facts of the Bible.

What has this to do with our cavern? Simply this. The atheist cannot even admit that a flood of global proportions once covered the land, or reached up to the tops of mountains. Even though fossils of fish lay atop every mountain range on the earth, including the Himalayas, the atheist will never accept that such catastrophes ever happened because the Bible records one such event. Now this event, a global flood of mammoth proportions, is recorded in virtually every tradition, country, and culture in the entire world. This fact alone is evidence that such an event once took place, but the atheist fears. Fear is their motive. Fear is what drives many men. It is fear that drives men to do what they might normally fear to do. This irony was to be Raja's fate. He was climbing down a cavern formed by flood water on one of the tallest mountains in the world, headed to a fate he did not know. Raja's plans were not God's. Raja had one plan, but God had another.

*****

As they entered the cave the light from the entrance shown only a few hundred feet. Those feet passed so very quickly that Raja was surprised when he found himself unable to see after such a short walk. Milton was still a few steps behind him, drawing breath slowly and deeply.

Raja bent over and dropped his backpack. Opening the backpack he pulled out what looked like a stick of dynamite, but this stick was of a different kind. It is easy to understand the confusion, but this was a flare. As he lit the flare, the cave lit up and he could see a huge room below him filled with various stalactites and stalagmites.

The stalactites were cave formations created by dripping water from the top of the cave. As the water drops down from the ceiling little bits of minerals, such as lime and calcium, are pulled down. The more water that drips, the larger the formation grows. At the bottom where the water hits the floor, there develops a mound formed from these mineral deposits. These are called stalagmites. Over the centuries, the mounds grow larger and the stalactites grow bigger until they meet and form a column.

Other columns include the "soda straws" which are a kind of stalactite but are formed as water flows through the inside of the formation like a thin straw. These formations usually get too heavy after time and break off as they are very thin, but regular stalactites simply grow bigger and wider and can support their own weight most of the time.

Various other formations, or "speleothems" as scientists call them, exist when water flows over these mineral deposits like a small waterfall, creating beautiful flowstones. Some of these formations have been variously called "cave bacon," because it looks like a strip of bacon hanging on a wall, "popcorn," and even "draperies."

Raja remembered getting into an argument with Milton over these formations once. As odd as it sounds, even such a simple thing as cave formations brought about a religious debate. Raja could never understand why. It was a *fact*, or so he thought, that these formations took hundreds of thousands of years to form. When he commented on the age of the cave, Milton informed him that he had once visited the famous Carlsbad Caverns and saw stalactites over six inches long hanging off of an exit sign. Had the exit sign been hanging there for thousands of years? This annoyed Raja, of course. It was most annoying because it was true. All geologists had to admit that there is no constant rate of growth for these formations. In theory they *could* have taken a hundred thousand years to form, but Milton insisted that a global flood, such as that described in the Bible, could have carved these caves and created many of the formations only a few thousand years ago. Raja said that was just assumption. Milton said the same of Raja's theory. Both were annoyed. Both were right.

"Even in destruction, God creates such beauty." Such were the words of Milton. He was referencing the belief that the cave was formed during this catastrophic flood in the days of Noah. Raja caught the reference, but chose to ignore it. There were more important things to do, such as finding their way down.

"So how do we get down from here?"

"I have no idea." There was a snicker as he said it, but he meant it. "The first time I just felt my way down and the way up there was only one way to go. If we go down the wrong way, we could fall into a bottomless pit."

Of course the pits weren't really bottomless, but they were deep enough drops to kill any man, and Raja was well aware of this. If he could not see the bottom with his flare, they would not risk it. This time at least they had some rope and rappelling equipment. They also had a map given to them by the monks, but the map was not easy to read. There were no clear markers and neither Milton nor Raja could make sense of most of it. It was better than nothing, and they could identify the big chambers on the map, but they would have to help one another if they were to reach the bottom.

"Well. It is a long journey, my friend. We can rest or start up now or go on," said Milton.

"Let's get going. We can rest on the way, but I don't want to waste any time."

*****

Two days had passed and they were still scaling down the caverns. Raja had brought plenty of flares, but he had not anticipated the duration and length of trip. He decided to alternate between flares and a flash light, but he knew the batteries would not last long either. The light from the flash light also was incapable of reaching as far as the flares, and thus slowed their descent as it made it harder to see whether or not they were heading in the right direction.

Occasionally, when the flare was exhausted there would be a moment of complete darkness. Raja had heard that if there was no light at all, total blackness, for a period of days at a time, a man would go completely blind, and he had even heard that a man could go insane. When he asked Milton about this, Milton replied as follows.

"The insanity claim is nonsense. Blind people are not insane and loosing sight may make us mad or filled with self pity, but it is ridiculous to claim that darkness can cause insanity, although I too have heard that argument. As to becoming completely blind, I can only say that cataracts can form if the eyes are removed from any light at all for an extended period of time, but a few days will not do it. To be sure, I was blinded by the light of the sun when I first exited the cave, and it was almost a week before I could really open my eyes and walk out in the sunlight again. Our eyes are very sensitive, but they are not so fragile as to die in a few days. We will be fine. Besides, the flares and flashlights are more than enough to keep our eyes active."

"Let's get some sleep. I am exhausted."

"Yea. I wonder what time it is."

"Good question. You loose sense of time without the sun." Raja pulled out his watch, which read 10 AM in the morning.

"Well, it is as good a time to sleep as any."

They both laughed a little as they were both tired, so they found a place to rest and camp out. A small campfire was started using equipment from their backpack.

"Want to eat something?" asked Raja.

"Yes. Thank you. Is this brunch or a midnight snack? I feels like midnight, but it is brunch time."

Raja smiled, but his mind was on something else. "You really don't know how much longer? Are you sure we will even find the exit this time? What if it was just dumb luck last time."

"There is no such thing as dumb luck."

Knowing to what, or rather to whom, Milton was referring, Raja said nothing. Milton just smiled and added, "you said you wanted to come."

"Which reminds me. Why did you let me come? I know you were against it from the start, but you gave in far too easily."

Milton chuckled a little. "Honestly?" He did not wait for an answer, "I need you Raja. I need someone to help me. My cancer is worse than I have told anyone and I was not sure I could make it back alone."

"So it is not because you trust me."

Milton smiled, "If I didn't trust you, I would have found someone else, but do you trust yourself? That is the question."

Raja was taken aback somewhat and let out a sharp, but short, laugh. "What? Of course!" Puzzled, he asked, "What does that mean?"

"You see Raja, it is not that I don't trust you and love you as a wayward brother. It is that I do not believe you know what you are getting into." Milton contemplated his next words, "Lord Acton once said,

'Power corrupts, and absolute power corrupts absolutely. Great men are almost always bad men.' And you, my friend, want to be great."

Raja wanted to laugh, for it is true that he wanted to be a great man. After all, who doesn't, he thought. Why would anyone not want to reach for greatness in whatever his field of endeavor. At first Raja was inclined to take this as a simpleton waiting for someone to lead him, but he knew Milton too well to believe that. Did Milton not want to be great? He finally asks, "Do you not want to be a great missionary?"

"I want to be the best I can be, but greatness should be about serving others, not ourselves. The truly great men of history were men who were humble and thought nothing of their legacy. Moses, Jesus, Washington. These were great men. Moses did not even want to lead the Exodus, but God commanded him to do so. Jesus gave everything for us. He could have been king, but laid it down along with His life that we might live eternal life. Washington was offered a kingship. Most people don't realize that, but he was offered a chance to be king of America and refused. Greatness lies in serving God and man, not ourselves."

"So you don't trust me ... not really."

"I trust with all my heart that God is in charge. I just pray that you will be on His side."

Raja was not getting irritated. He rolled his eyes and ignored what he perceived as a personal slight. Instead his mind drifted to curiosity. "How did these people come to be? I mean, a valley of the blind?"

"I don't know, but from the looks of their eyes I would guess that the first explorer to the valley suffered from some sort of glaucoma. Perhaps it was passed on too their children genetically or perhaps there is something in the valley itself that is harmful to the eyes. Some sulphite or compound that caused blindness, but how it could come to affect the children I do not know. That would imply some sort of genetic mutation."

"Mutation? Hmmmm." This innocent thought was about to start another debate, although Raja had not intended it.

Milton replied, "I know what you are thinking but no truly beneficial mutation has ever been observed in the hundreds of years of research. Moreover, even if such a thing occurred, it would not, and could not, create new species. Genetic Reproductive Isolation is the scientific definition of species and using that criteria, no new species have ever been observed to arise in all the time we have been researching them."

"But they have arisen using taxonomical definitions," mumbled Raja.

"Yes, but even Thomas Huxley admitted that taxonomy uses 'completely arbitrary' definitions. Genetics was discovered by a monk about the same time as Darwin was formulating his 'scientific' application of the ancient theory."

"Ancient?"

"Yes, evolution actually stems from eastern religion and concepts. Because they view the universe itself as god, it is a living and evolving entity, but you knew that."

Raja just smiled and decided to let Milton continue his diatribe. This was nice since, although Raja did not realize it at the time, it was to be their last debate. Even in Milton's scratchy voice it was clear that Milton was exerting effort just to speak. That is one reason Raja did not antagonize him.

"Anyway, a poor man's comparison might be to compare the gene pool for a larger species (or at least genus) to a deck of playing cards. You might be dealt a full house, a straight, a flush, four of a kind, or even be stuck with an 8 high. The deck is the same for everyone who is playing, but each set of cards are different. If you have a straight and marry a girl with a flush, you might have a son with a straight flush."

Raja couldn't help but smile, even though he knew Milton's thesis was a shot at Darwinism.

"Over time, as people or animals spread out over the globe, you might see people who only have clubs or diamonds, so it might appear that they are a different race from us, but if we can produce living offspring, it is proof that we are from the same larger gene pool. This is what is meant by Genetic Reproductive Isolation. Two different species cannot produce living offspring. If you take the semen from a dog and implant a cat egg, you will not have a cog or a dat, because they are playing with a different deck ..."

Raja mumbled under his breath, "sometimes I think you aren't playing with a full deck," but he meant in as a friendly jest.

"No my friend, I do not believe that maggots, slugs, and cock roaches are my distant cousins. Nor have any transitional fossils been found to show those 'walking fish' you see on the back of atheists' cars."

Raja laughed out loud. "The Darwin stickers you mean?"

"Yes. It is meant to mock the Jesus stickers which show the Christian symbol of a fish. They, of course, have Darwin's name, and a fish with feet, but when have you ever seen a fish with feet? Have you ever seen a fossil of one?"

"Amphibians."

"But an amphibian has a respiratory system in advance of both fish and mammals as it can breath both above and below water. It cannot be an ancestor to what it is advanced of, and not a single solitary fossil of any such transitional creature exist. Dinosaurs likewise cannot be a missing link as they require even more transitions, which are likewise 'missing.'"

"Milton ..."

"Am I annoying you?"

"Yes," Raja replied with a smile.

"Sorry. I guess my point is that whatever caused their blindness cannot affect us. I have lived here for ten years and have experienced no ill effects. I can see fine. Whatever the cause, it must be long gone or strictly a genetic disorder."

Milton immediately begins to cough and doubled over in pain. Raja got up and moved over to pat him on the back. He really didn't even know what to do, but it was instinctive to show concern and pat him on the back.

To this Milton raised his hand slowly, saying, "Thank you my friend but I am fine. It is my cancer.

Nothing else." He paused to catch his breath and then continued, "Yes Raja, I am paying for my sins all those years ago. I smoked cigarettes for twenty years before I quit. The irony is that I quit when I found this valley simply because they had no tobacco. I have been clean for these past ten years, but my lifestyle caught up with me."

Again Raja mumbled under his breath. He did not intend to be heard, but he forgot that the caverns made echoes and the acoustics made it very hard not to be heard. There were no background noises and it was silent as outer space save the occasional dripping of water from the ceilings. Consequently, it was no surprise that Milton heard his simple comment, "So much for your loving God."

To this Milton felt obligated to respond. "No Raja. No. I knew what smoking did. We have all known. Can you blame God because we don't want to accept responsibility? If we run a red light and get in a car wreck can you blame God? I don't. I will be with the Lord, preparing a place for my beloved Angel-i."

Milton drifted off into dreams of his wife. Raja, realizing that Milton would not be around to debate in the near future, made a half-hearted attempt at apologizing, saying, "I'm sorry Jim, I just don't care much for intolerant religions."

"Intolerant?"

"You believe everyone who doesn't think like you goes to hell, right?"

Milton broke out into laughter, stopped only by his sore and bleeding throat. "Oh ... *that*," he said sarcastically, "no, Raja. We believe that anyone from *any* background, from *any* ethnicity, from *any* religion, or *any* culture can repent and trust in the Lord Jesus and be saved without having to live a thousand lifetimes or whatever else some require. Is that so intolerant?"

Raja, realizing he had gone to far, resorted to the old time tested method of getting out of a bad situation he was obviously loosing; he changed the topic. "Wake me when are you ready to resume. It is so cold in here I doubt I will get much rest anyway."

They did not realize it, but this was to be the last argument they would ever have. Raja had unconsciously missed being challenged by Milton and it is, perhaps, for that reason that seemed to push him so hard this day. He regretted it, but he would regret it all the more tomorrow, for as we often do, we forget that tomorrow is never guaranteed. We should love our friends and family and neighbors as if there is no tomorrow, for we never know how many days God has allotted to us. We must instead choose not to waste those allotted days, but to make a difference for Him in these short days we have been given.

*****

The next day they continued their journey down the cave. It had been almost six hours when they heard a loud cry. It was the cry of an animal and gave both of them a jolt. Milton, at first startled, quickly lightened up the atmosphere, saying, "It is the Yeti!"

Raja just looked at Milton and laughed, but Milton could not return the laugh as he again doubled

94

over in a coughing fit. Blood began to seep from his mouth, but he recovered soon.

"Come my, friend. The exit can't be far now for no animal ventures this far into the cave unless there is an exit nearby."

After another hour, they could see the light from the entrance. Raja was ecstatic. "Look! Light! It is coming from somewhere down there!"

Panting for breath Milton only said, "Slow down. Don't get too excited. It is still hours away. In as place a dark as this, light can travel a long way."

"Yes yes. I won't leave you, my friend. But hours or not. I don't want to rest until we get there!"

With that they began the final descent, but Milton was unable to take more than a few steps at a time. He was wheezing and coughing constantly. Raja wrapped his arm around Milton and helped to carry him for much of the way. Finally, not two hundred yards from the exit, Milton collapsed.

"Hang on, Jim! We are almost there!"

"I just want to see my Angel-i before I die."

Raja realized that this was the only reason Milton returned at all. He had looked deafly pale even when they had met back at the Hotel Dallas, but Raja had secretly wondered why his friend brought him. He knew Milton needed help to get back, and yet he had feigned not wanting Raja to come all along. What if Raja had agreed not to come? Would Milton have made it? Would that monk (Raja did not even think his name from sheer contempt) have helped him? Finally, realizing how close they were to the exit, Raja discarded his equipment, knowing it would not be hard to come back for, and carried Milton in both his arms.

As they came to the exit of the cave, the moonlight was blinding enough, but not overly so. Had it been daylight, Raja might not have been able to carry Milton outside at all. Unlike Milton's original trip, they did have flares and flashlights, although the batteries had run out two days before. Consequently, Raja's eyes were unaccustomed to bright light, but not so much as to make light painful as had been the case with Milton before.

The last few dozen yards were like finishing a race. There was a sense of relief and exhaustion all rolled into one. Walking into the moonlight was like walking into the bright sun after sitting in a dark movie theater for a double feature. Raja fell to his knees with a barely conscious Milton in his arms. They had finally made it to the Valley.

9 – A Brief Reunion

"Hallooooooo! Halloooooo!"

Raja shouted out to anyone that could hear. He assumed that most of the people were asleep as it was nighttime, but he wondered if a blind civilization even took note of the day and night. Obviously they could feel the heat of the sun, but that might actually mean that they would prefer to work in the cool of the night and sleep in the hot of the day. In either case, asleep or awake, Raja made sure that they could hear him.

"I need help here! *Bacchaoo*!" The later word is, Raja assumed, a Hindi word meaning "help" but his Hindi was practically non-existent so he just hoped that it was something close.

Finally a tall man emerged around a bend. Raja could not see what was behind the bend in the mountain, but there soon followed several men behind this tall man. Their eyes were all, as Milton had said, milky white. It gave Raja an eerie feeling to see this in the dead of night. Thoughts of bad horror films and zombie movies flashed through his head briefly, but soon faded as more important things were at hand.

"*Kya*? *Kaun hai*?" said the elderly tall man.

The others were also speaking, but Raja could not make out any of the words. He replied in English, "Milton is ill! He needs help!"

"Milton?" said the old man, now speaking in English, "Come! Our friend has returned and is in need of help!"

Several others shouted frantically while the elder man approached quickly, but his steps were careful. The walk was odd, as if he wanted to run but was afraid of hitting something he could not see. Therefore he took long strides as if he were trying to kick something which was not there, but the foot would then step down safely and his other foot would follow the same pattern. It was almost amusing to Raja were it not for the circumstances. Eventually, a young woman came running, and she was running; not concerned with falling at all. She shouted out, "Jim!"

Having heard Anjali's voice, the barely conscious Milton uttered out, "My Angel, I am here." As she fell upon him, he looked up at his young beautiful bride and said, "I see an angel."

Now these were the last words that Raja ever heard from his old friend. The men quickly picked him up and carried him off towards a village which Raja could not yet see, as it was hidden around the bend of the mountains surrounding the valley. The valley itself seemed quite large, but the cliff faces were sheer vertical drops. It was hard for Raja to concentrate. His five senses were being assaulted all at once. The beauty of the valley was like nothing he had seen before although he was still having a hard time adjusting his eyes. The sounds of men shouting in a foreign language and panicking at Milton's state shook Raja's nerves. His own feelings were a mixture of awe, fear, sorrow, and joy. Even the smell of pollen from nearby was strong, almost as if he had never smelled pollen before at all. Finally, even his lips tasted salty from being parched for they had rationed their food as best they could to insure they reached the valley.

With all these senses pressing on Raja's brain he almost didn't notice that the tall elderly man who had spoken English did not leave with the others who were carrying Milton away. Raja turned to look at the man who seemed to be staring right through him. Raja had spoken and was shuffling his feet ever so slightly. Obviously, it was apparent that he was there and that the man knew it. He realized that he was being quite rude, so Raja immediately spoke up.

"Where are they taking Jim?"

"To Jiven, our doctor."

"I would like to come," Raja said out of respect.

"Yes, but first," there was a tone of suspicion in his voice, "who are you?"

"My name is Raja Sinha. I am Milton's friend and colleague."

"I am called Pita-ji, because I am the father of this valley and these people. Jim said nothing of bringing anyone back with him." His words seemed both cold and stern.

"He needed me. He could not make the journey by himself, as you can see." Raja had unconsciously added those final words as a simple figure of speech.

"See?"

Pita-ji's tone send a shiver down Raja's spine. He remembered what Milton had told him. It is unlikely the people of the valley even knew what the word "see" meant, but the tone in Pita-ji's voice suggested otherwise, and it was a tone of disappointment and distrust.

"We shall hear of this later," said Pita-ji. "Let us attend our friend."

Raja took note of the idiom, "we shall hear of this" rather than "we shall see." At least this is how Raja interpreted the words. He took it as a challenge of sorts. Raja was a stubborn man with a bit of a temper and he did not like Pita-ji's tone or suspicions, and he was *sure* that it was a suspicion of his motives. "We shall see if you are telling the truth." *That* is what Pita-ji meant.

Pita-ji took a step back, turning slightly to the side and did not move. Raja was curious what this signified and stood there staring at him, looking into his vacant white eyes staring into the distance.

"Come," said Pita-ji, as if he had expected Raja to do something.

Raja realized he was being invited to follow the men to the valley, and began to walk off in the direction which he had seen them carry his friend. Pita-ji heard his footsteps and followed close behind, giving occasional instructions, like "to your right." Raja wisely did not say what he was thinking, namely, "I can see," although the temptation was great and more than once he found himself about to utter those very words, but caught himself before hand. Instead, he said, "thank you."

*****

As they rounded the bend, Raja could now see the village. It was really a city; a small city, but a city nevertheless. There were, however, no buildings save a large stone dome in the center. Aside from the dome there was not even a simple hut. Instead it was like a tiny city of Petra. The homes were carved into the sides of the cliff faces. The houses had a simple opening for a door, but no actual door to close. Likewise there were no windows of any kind. At first, Raja cynically thought they were cavemen, but what struck his eye the most was the sophisticated system of streets. Yes, there were streets in the tiny village. The roads were variously paved with different substances. Some were made of straw, others of gravel, and still others of sand. Small as the city was there were several intersections and in the center of those intersections were large poles with something hanging on it. This intrigued Raja.

"What could be hanging from a blind man's street sign," he thought to himself. As they approached, he saw that the one closest to him had several large and pungent peppers hanging from it. He was about to asks what its purpose was when Pita-ji spoke.

"Turn left at the signpost."

"Signpost," thought Raja. Yes, it is just that! Smell! They could smell what street they were on. Raja began to giggle, much to Pita-ji's dismay.

"What is so funny at a time like this?" he barked.

Realizing that his friend lay quite possibly dying at this very moment, Raja tried his best to make an excuse, for he knew they would never understand, or appreciate, the truth.

"I am sorry. I just feel happy for Jim that we made it back. It is his dying wish to see his family before he dies."

"See?? Dies??" Pita-ji was clearly angry now and Raja knew he was only putting his foot in his mouth, so he said nothing more. Pita-ji, the village elder, did not press the issue, but told Raja to slow down. He then moved ahead and walked in front.

"Follow me."

Less than a minute later, they arrived at the entrance to a cave with a simple carved doorway. It was a human carved cave, but nothing ornate or special. The doorway was smooth and shaped like any other doorway, but the absence of any windows or light source made it very eerie. Raja stood, therefore, at the entrance of the cave while Pita-ji entered.

The cave, whatever it was, was very crowded. Many people were inside when Raja heard someone shouting. "Everyone out! I can't work here." Raja made way to allow the visitors to leave. It was apparent that this was their hospital, or at least the doctor's house. Milton lay inside with the doctor and his bride, Anjali.

The village elder emerged from the house last and spoke in a loud voice, "Milton-ji has returned, but he may not be with us for long. Go back to sleep. Jiven will do what he can."

Raja stood by, afraid to say anything, but his eye was caught but a beautiful young woman. Her hair was jet black as the night, and her skin was lightly tanned. She stood about five feet three inches from the ground and had a dainty, but not skinny, body. He regretted that he could not see more for she was dressed modestly in a drab dark gray sari which did not accentuate her breasts, making it hard for Raja to judge her assets. Of course, blind people would not naturally show off cleavage for those who cannot see, but the mystery somehow made her even more attractive to Raja. He had seen many beautiful women before, but something about this girl struck him. She was obviously not made up or painted and did not flaunt her body. Such eye tantalizing was not needed here, nor did Raja believe that she needed makeup or artificial enhancements, although he did find himself wishing that the valley was a little warmer. Perhaps she wouldn't be wearing as many clothes, he thought to himself. These thoughts were soon interrupted by the gruff voice of authority.

"Is that man still here or did he leave?"

"I am here. Where would I go?" replied a frustrated Raja. He was not feeling welcome.

"Forgive me. You cannot hear Milton-ji now. He is gravely ill."

"Cannot *hear* him now," thought Raja? Again the idioms of the valley were strangely humorous to him. Surely he meant that he could not *see* him now. Raja smiled to himself, but kept his laughter inside, especially given the solemn nature of the events which were transpiring. "I understand," was Raja's reply.

"Come, I will take you to your guest house."

The house was about five doors down. He entered the pitch black room with only the faintest of light coming from the moon and shining through a single doorway. He tried to feel his way to the bed, but stubbed his toe in the process. He had expected a full sized bed about two feet off the ground, but instead there was just a mat, which is what he tripped over, falling clumsily down upon the low lying mat. Honestly, he didn't even care. He was dead tired and all the events that had transpired only made him more weary. It was already late in the night, probably around one or two in the morning. He rolled over on his back and looked out the door to see the elder was still there, standing.

"Are you okay?" he asked.

"Yes. I am fine. Thank you." Raja almost forgot himself again was about to say, "I just didn't see the bed," but thought better of it.

Pita-ji then turned and walked off after saying "good night." Raja didn't see which way he went, and didn't care. He fell fast asleep, but remained restless from worry about his friend. Moreover, it was only five hours later that he was awakened with sobering, but not unexpected, news.

"Our friend Milton-ji has ascended."

10 – The Stranger

The sun had barely risen, and Raja was commanded to appear before the council. He wondered at first why a blind people should bother to rise with the sun, but he knew better. They could feel the warmth of the sun and had some livestock, such as chickens, which he had not noticed last night. Day and night were more than the absence or presence of light. Raja knew this in his head, and yet his mind did not fully absorb it. Things he took for granted he realized were not taken so by the valley people.

Raja was escorted to the only structure in the village. All the other houses and shops were carved into the rocks like caves. Only the village council chamber lay in the middle of the tiny city. It was made of rocks almost like a giant igloo. There were no windows and only one doorway. As Raja entered it was very dark, for the mountains shielded the sun and the door lay on the west, so that there was only a little light gleaming in from the entrance.

"*Aaja.* Come. Sit. We have grave news, and there is much to discuss." It was Pita-ji speaking. His voice was not as stern as last night, but he spoke as one with authority. Nevertheless, Raja detected some sympathy in his voice.

"Yes. Thank you."

Raja tried to find his seat but there was nothing. The men were sitting on the floor much as the American Indians did, with legs crossed, but Raja could not tell this until his eyes became adjusted to the dark. He was not helped by the fact that a crowd had gathered around the entrance to the council chamber, blocking what little light there was. He actually found himself inadvertently kicking one man, and nearly falling over another. In both cases he apologized profusely.

"Sit where you are," said a dwarf. Raja could barely make him out in the darkness, but he was clearly a dwarf. He thought this odd at first, but having taught science he quickly realized that dwarfism can be caused by genetic disorders such as Growth hormone deficiency. These hormones, or somatotropins, stimulate the growth of cells. Thus their deficiency causes many cells to remain stagnant and not grow. Still it was unusual, Raja thought, to see a dwarf siting upon a council. He could not think of a single politician in his lifetime who was a dwarf.

Raja followed orders and sat down quietly. It was Pita-ji who spoke first.

"I presume you received the sad news?"

"Yes. Jim is dead."

"We all grieve our friend."

There was a round of agreement by all within the council and by those outside who were clearly listening at the doorway.

Pita-ji continued, "we will hold the funeral rite this evening. You, of course, will come."

"Yes. I shall. He was a good friend and colleague."

Another man introduced himself. He was elderly and somewhat frail. As he was sitting down it was hard to judge his height, but Raja figured he was about the same height as himself. "I am Salah. The *dusura* of the council. We know that this is not the appropriate time to question you, and we shall reconvene the council in a few days after the funeral and after you have had some time to acquaint yourself with our village and people."

"Thank you. I understand."

"However," he spoke not angrily, but as one who had been interrupted, "there are some preliminary questions we must ask."

"And some rules you must know," said the unnamed dwarf.

"Yes, yes. One at a time." Pita-ji said. "First, tell us of what happened with Milton-ji for he transpired before he could tell us about you."

Raja was a little taken aback by the statement. Had Milton died so soon? Was Milton already dead when they took him to the doctor's house? If so, why did they say nothing until this morning? Were they hiding something? These thoughts rushed through his head in no particular order. Finally, he responded guardedly, "Well, Jim returned to the real world," he instantly knew this was a stupid choice of words but pretended not to have said them, "and consulted with the doctors, but his cancer had progressed too far. There was no way they could have saved his life, so he chose to return here to his new home and die with his family."

Suddenly he heard the sound of crying erupt behind him. As he turned and looked, he saw a woman leaving the chamber in tears. Although it was too dark to tell, he assumed that the woman was Anjali. After a short pause, Pita-ji said, "Please continue. How did you come to be here?"

"Well, I brought him ..."

Immediately he was interrupted as if he had said something offensive. It was Salah. "You *brought* him?" There was a curious emphasis on the word "brought."

"Well, yes."

"So he did not bring you," said the dwarf.

"It is the same thing!" Raja was now defensive, but it was Pita-ji who calmed the storm.

He said, "Please. We must all introduce ourselves when we first speak as he does not know any of us."

"Yes, my apologies. I am Manish," said the dwarf. "I am the *tisara* here."

Of course Raja had no idea what the titles meant, but he understood that these were the leaders of the tribe. Pita-ji was clearly the village elder, and Salah and Manish were apparently his lieutenants or advisors.

"Pleased to meet you."

"Please understand," said Salah, "Milton-ji died without speaking about you and he had always promised never to betray the secret of the valley."

"We must be sure of your honor and intentions," said Manish.

"I assure you. I came as a friend of Jim. He was clearly too ill and sick to make the journey by himself. He wanted to see his wife before he died, so I," Raja paused, choosing his words carefully, "came with him to insure he made the trip safely. I also promised to help you people."

"Help us?" said Salah, "So you are a missionary too?"

"Please. I doubt the existence of some God."

"So you are a missionary who does not believe in God. Your friend led you here but never mentioned you. And you want to help. Is that right?" was Manish's response.

Raja grunted his own reply but no words could be comprehended.

"Anjali!" called out Pita-ji.

There was some mumbling behind Raja. He could hear people saying "Ahhh oh! Ahh oh!" This he thought was quite odd, until he later learned that "*aao*" was a *hindi* word meaning "come."

Soon Anjali, still wiping tears from her eyes, appeared in the doorway. "*Ji?*"

"*Aao. Baitho,*" said Pita-ji.

She moved and carefully sat down without so much as bumping anyone. For the moment Raja reserved questioning how she could do this, which for him seemed a major feat.

"*Ye hamare mehmaan hai. kripya inse angreji me baat kare,*" were the strange words which came from Pita-ji's mouth.

"Yes sir," she replied.

"Anjali. This man, who calls himself Raja Sinha, claims to be a friend of Milton-ji. Please, think carefully. Did Sir James ever speak of him to you?"

Raja was almost as curious to hear the answer as were the other council members. Did Milton remember him all these many years?

"Yes. I remember he spoke of Raja." There was a sigh of relief in Raja's heart for many reasons, but Anjali continued. "I also remember that he was the one with whom Jim had traveled when he was lost and found his way to the valley."

"Interesting," said Manish. "How did he come to be lost?"

"Surely he has told us many times, Manish," there was a soft scolding in Anjali's soft voice. "It was an accident. Raja must have assumed that Jim was dead. A search party could never have found him."

"Yes yes," said Pita-ji. "Thank you. We will speak with you more in private. For now that is all."

Anjali got up and walked over to a corner. Again, Raja wondered how she never bumped into anyone, but he also noticed that which he had not before. The people around her was shuffling their feet deliberately as if warning her of their presence. She could hear the feet shuffle and navigated around them as surely as if she could see them. Raja was somewhat astounded but the situation gave him no time to think upon these matters.

"Are there any further questions," asked Pita-ji.

"Just one," said Salah. "Please forgive us, but when you entered here you fell over someone and kicked another. Are you ill?"

Somewhat embarrassed, Raja simply, and wisely replied, "I am just shaken by news of my friends' death."

"I hear," replied Salah.

"I simply didn't see him."

"*Kya?*" said Manish.

"English," reminded Pita-ji.

"You said you didn't what?"

"I didn't see him."

"See?" said Salah.

Anjali saved Raja from further embarrassment by speaking up, "remember their language is different from ours. It is a word Jim sometimes spoke until we forbade it. It simply means that he did not hear them."

"Ahh, of course," said Salah, but there was a little doubt in his voice. There was more doubt in Raja's mind. Why did they "forbid" him to use such a simple word?

"Are their any other questions," asked Pita-ji.

"Not now. Later I shall have many," said Manish.

"So be it." Pita-ji now addressed Raja. "We will reconvene another day. In the meantime you will find plenty to explore outside. I will assign Rani to guide you through our village until the funeral rite."

Pita-ji then clapped his hands together and called out, "Rani!" Shortly thereafter, a woman appeared in the door way. Raja's eyes were now accustomed enough to the light to be able to make out the woman standing in the doorway. It was the same beautiful woman he had noticed last night! Suddenly, calmness settled over Raja and replied, "I would be delighted to have someone so lovely show me around."

This comment was greeted by strange expressions. It was clear that the people did not understand his words. Finally, Rani spoke up in a husky, but pleasant voice, saying, "Thank you, but how do you know I am lovely since we have never spoken before?" There was a bit of a giggle, but before Raja could even answer, she said, "I know you are just being kind, sir. Thank you."

Raja was about to speak when Anjali interrupted him. "Sir. I am sure that Raja-ji is very exhausted from his travels and experience. Perhaps he should be dismissed so we can talk."

"Yes indeed," said Pita-ji. "Rani will guide you. Go with her. We have to speak with Anjali."

With this Raja thanked everyone and got up to leave. He walked over to Rani, but was not entirely sure how to approach a blind woman. It was obvious that he said many things which made the council leery of him, and he did not want to drive Rani off, so he simply said, "Shall we go."

"*Ji haan*. Yes. Come. *Aao*."

As Raja left, Anjali came and sat down in his place. It is clear that she wanted to speak on his behalf, but not in front of him.

"Speak," said Pita-ji.

"Jim did speak of Raja sometimes. I do not fully understand their relationship, but they were friends."

"What is there that you do not understand?" asked Manish.

"They argued all the time and Jim would often speak of Raja's temper, stubbornness, and other poor character traits and yet he always defended Raja."

"That is indeed hard to understand," it was Pita-ji who spoke, "and very enlightening. Please go on."

"Well, they knew each other for a very long time. Jim would say that he liked to be challenged and that Raja kept him on his toes, because they had

112

very different beliefs. Particularly when it came to God."

Pita-ji laughed. "We had those arguments as well, I remember."

"No no. Hindus believe in God. Christians and Hindus have very different conceptions of God, but we all still believe in God."

"You mean this Raja truly does not believe in God!" This time it was Manish who spoke out, as did several other onlisteners. He had heard Raja's remark about "doubting" God but was shocked to hear that he did not really believe in God.

"No. He thinks of man as the ultimate being in the universe. I do not believe he will ever cause us physical harm, but he does tend to look down upon the religions of men. It is common among western agnostics and even eastern communists."

"We am not familiar with these terms you use," reminded Salah.

"Yes, forgive me. They are factions in his world."

"It seems a strange world," lamented Pita-ji.

"Yes it is."

Pita-ji now spoke up more sternly, "What is really important is whether or not we can trust him. You know we cannot risk the safety of this valley. We are too few."

"Yes I understand. From what Jim told me, I do not believe he would have brought him here if he were not trustworthy."

"Are you sure he brought Raja here?" The voice came from Jiven, the village doctor.

"Yes. I believe so."

There was silence for a brief time. Finally, Pita-ji spoke, "are there any more questions?"

"Just one," said Salah. "When he entered the hut he acted as clumsy as a new born child, unable to even walk across a room. Do you know why?"

"Remember, our world is different and this place is unfamiliar to him. I am sure that he get used to it given time."

"Does he have hearing problems or some other physical ailment?"

"I do not know."

"Very well then," said Pita-ji. "We shall discuss this and keep an ear on Sinha. After the funeral tomorrow we shall give him a day or two of mourning and then recall him when we shall decide what to do with him. Until then, treat him with all the respect and courtesy due a stranger. The guest is god in our house, remember."

11 – First Impressions

Rani guided Raja around the village. I cannot say that she "showed" him the village, for she did not believe in sight. How could she believe in what she had never known? Even Anjali sometimes doubted her husband, although that doubt was usually only momentary. No, Rani guided Raja and gave him a tour of their small city; nothing more.

As they walked down a pathway, they came to a large "sign." It was a post with onions hanging in a basket.

"This is Onion Street," she explained. "This leads to our gardens. Come, this way."

Rani walked on the west; near the cliffs. Raja followed closely, but his eyes were transfixed on her more than anything else. This was no small irony for the valley surrounding him was beautiful. It seemed untouched and natural as God had made it.

Rani continued to explain, "I imagine your people use similar methods, but in case they are different I should explain. Roads with sand indicate a path to food. Gardens, livestock farms, and the banquet area. We had planned such a wonderful banquet for Milton-ji's return. It is such as shame."

"What is this 'ji' you say after every name?" inquired Raja.

Rani giggled a little but answered politely. "It is term of respect. Milton-ji taught some of us your language. The closest translation would be 'sir,' except that we place it after the name, rather than before it. It is not considered polite to be too familiar with someone unless they are your relative. Only family members refer to Milton-ji by his first name."

"So you are Rani-ji?"

A broad smile crossed her lips, and it made Raja happy as well. "Yes, you may call me Rani-ji. Perhaps one day I shall even let you call me Rani." She quickly turned away and continued down the path. Finally, remembering where she left off, she continued her explanation. "Oh yes. Sand is for food. Gravel leads to the main Council Chambers. Wood chips lead to our homes. Dirt roads usually lead out into the valley. Leaves indicate a warning track. When you feel leaves under your feet, you know you are at the edge of the road."

Somehow this fascinated Raja. "It is amazing how you are able to do all this."

"Do what?"

"Well, I mean I would never have thought of this."

"Thought of what?"

"The sand and leaves and pungent plants to mark road signs. It is quite, well," he was struggling with his words, "it takes a lot of ingenuity."

"Why? How do you do it in your society?"

"Well we just have concrete roads and written signs," he said.

"Written signs? You mean you have to stop at every post and feel the words?" She was, of course, referring to a sort of Braille which was used in the valley, although Raja did not catch the reference.

"What? No. We can see, you see?"

Why Raja suddenly decided to discuss his eyesight is not great a mystery. He liked Rani and he intended to help the people of the valley with his sight. He could not keep it a secret forever. Milton was too cautious. Besides, with Rani on his side, she could help convince the others of his usefulness. This was the thinking behind his decision.

"See? What is that?"

Raja was stricken at first. He knew that Milton had not discussed sight extensively because of his childish fears, but had they never even heard of sight?

"It is a fifth sense. You see, you have four senses. You can touch or feel, smell, taste, and hear. I can see as well."

"What does this 'see' do?"

"Well, I can tell what something is from far away. I do not have to be close enough to touch or smell it. For example," Raja looks around, "there. That is a bird up there on the cliff."

Rani smiled. "Oh you are teasing."

"No I am not."

"How do I know there is a bird there unless it chirps, and if it chirps I can hear it." She laughs and give Raja a playful slap. Does this 'see' make you clumsy too? I heard you twice stumble in the Council chambers."

"Well, it was dark."

"Dark?"

"Yes. The absence of light. I can't see in the dark."

Rani laughed at Raja and turned to run a few steps away. She then stopped, and turned back to Raja, shouting, "Come on! Can't you 'see' where I am going?"

Raja was a little annoyed, but not much. He would have ample opportunity to prove that he had a fifth sense, so he ran after Rani. Not a hundred yards away they came to a chicken coop.

"Oh chickens," said Raja. "Are you not vegetarians?"

"Some of us are, but some of us eat meat as well."

"And what about fruits and vegetables? Do you grow those here?" Raja knew the answer, of course, but he was being playful with Rani, who responded in kind.

"No silly. This is a chicken coop. We grow vegetables in the garden."

"And do you water them as well?"

"Of course."

"What about when it rains? Do you water them then?"

Giggling again, she said, "No not when it rains."

"Why not?"

"Because God is watering them, of course."

"Oh ... Him again." The instinctive reaction was quickly suppressed, but not before Rani caught wind of it. Milton had been a very religious man, but Raja did not like God? Most curious, she thought to herself.

"Show me the garden, please," said Raja, hoping to change the subject from God before it even got started.

"Show you? You have such funny words," she said while giggling.

"What?"

"See, look, show, watch." She starts to giggle again.

"Yes. Uh, guide me."

"Oh, yes." She turned around and walked up the path another dozen yards or more and then knelt down beside a large lush garden.

"Come. Here. Sit."

Raja felt like a dog but obliged anyway. How could he refuse her? He kneeled beside her. There were various fruits and vegetables in the garden. He recognized curry leaves, onions, garlic cloves, various chili peppers, dates, tomatoes, and even Honey Mangoes, although he thought those were indigenous to Pakistan.

"Oh, are those Honey Mangoes over there?"

Rani appeared surprised at first, for he was not close enough to smell them, and she had not mentioned them, but after a second of thinking, she let out a great laugh. She was laughing at him again! "Milton-ji told you about our gardens before. Didn't he?"

"No. I can see the mangoes from here."

Rani just giggled, and continued talking as if he had said nothing, "the garden is a little thin now because we have begun to harvest the fruits and vegetables this month. What kind of fruits do you grow?"

"Well, we have the usual." Raja was no connoisseur of fruits and vegetables, despite his love of Honey Mangoes, so he could only say, "I just buy whatever is at the market."

"Market?"

119

"Yes. We don't usually grow our own food. We let someone else do it for us, and he brings the food to the market."

"Why would you want someone else to do your work for you?"

Somehow, as much as Raja loved speaking to Rani, he felt that he was saying too much. She clearly did not believe him about eyesight, and now she was questioning such simple things as why no one grows their own food? He decided to make his apologies. "I am sorry. Jim died just last night. I am not feeling myself. Would you escort me back to my house. I didn't get much sleep last night, I am very tired."

"Of course. Follow me." Rani walked off toward the houses. Naturally, Raja could get back there on his own but he wanted an excuse to spend more time with Rani, so the trip back to the house was pleasant. When they arrived he wished her well, and told her he would take a nap.

"Yes, I am sure you will be excused from work under the circumstances. If you will excuse me."

Raja took note of the words, but said nothing. Obviously they expected him to work, and he was not adverse to it, but he wanted to lead, not follow. There was much weighing on Raja's mind now. A nap would be best, and given the long trip down the cavern, his biological clock had become altered as if he was suffering from jet lag. Consequently, he lay down and slept for nearly six more hours until the sun was directly overhead.

Raja awoke after noon. It was not wholly unusual for him, but this time he awoke refreshed without a headache. He left his stone carved house-cave and looked around the village. Much of the village seemed deserted at this time of day. Raja deduced that they were making preparations for the funeral, so he headed to the banquet area and there saw Rani and Anjali cutting fruits and vegetables.

"Greetings," he said.

Rani cocked her head toward Raja. "Oh, it's you. Greetings. Did you sleep well?"

"Yes, I little better. Thank you."

Rani and Anjali continued their work as Raja continued his dialogue, "I must say you people get along quite well."

"Of course. Why wouldn't we?" Raja detected a slight offense in her voice, but only slight.

"Sorry, I meant no offense. It is just that I would not be able to get around without eyesight as well as you."

Several people nearby cocked their heads, but said nothing. It was Anjali who spoke first. "Remember Rani, the believe they have a fifth sense."

"No, I hadn't heard before today. I was just a child when Milton-ji came. Tell me."

"I told you," said a bemused, and somewhat amused, Raja.

"It is best not to speak of this," said Anjali.

"Speak of what?" The voice was that of Pita-ji.

"A fifth sense. I thought Raja-ji was joking, but Anjali said he is serious. Do these people really have a fifth sense?" inquired Rani.

"I don't know. Do you?" The retort sounded like more of a challenge by Pita-ji than a question, but Raja decided to stand firm.

"Of course we do. I will prove it to you in due time."

There was silence for a moment when Raja himself broke the silence. "Now is not the time. My friend has passed away and is not even buried yet."

"Buried?" asked Rani.

Anjali answered for him, saying, "Yes, in their culture they bury their dead under the ground." She turned toward Raja and said, "but here we have a funeral pyre and send his ashes back to God. I am sure my husband would have approved."

"Yes, that is acceptable."

"Good," said Pita-ji. "We shall speak of this 'fifth sense' when we convene the council in a day or two. In the meantime, make yourself at home."

Pita-ji turned and walked away without another word. Perhaps he was not so angry as Raja had first thought. Perhaps Milton was just a little paranoid. They did not understand his eyesight so it is natural that they would be a little scared, but in time they would understand. He would not longer be feared but respected and even honored.

Raja's thoughts drifted to Cortez who was thought a god when he first landed upon the shores of Cancun, Mexico. Was he the new Cortez? His thoughts soon turned back to Rani.

"What are you making?"

"We are preparing a feast. It was to be a feast for Milton's return, but now we have a funeral, and the next day we have a somber feast for you."

"I understand. Thank you. What time will the funeral be?"

"After work hours, we shall rest and make the final preparations. It shall be shortly before dinner, although no one will feel much like eating."

"Thank you again. I will see you later."

As Raja walked off, Rani turned toward Anjali and asked, "'See me later?' What does that mean?"

"Even their idioms seem to relate to their fifth sense. Jim spoke of it to me, but it was not something we were proud of, so we never spoke of it openly. It makes people feel odd, and many thought Jim insane until he ceased talking about it. I am sure it will be the same with Raja."

"Do you believe there is such a thing?"

"No," said Pita-ji who was now standing behind them. "When we first met Milton-ji there was a language barrier, but when we learned each other's language, we realized their 'fifth sense' was nothing more than 'feelings' or 'deja vu.' Is that not right, Anjali?"

"Yes sir."

Pita-ji turned back to Rani, "Do you think he likes you?"

"I don't know. Why?"

"I think he likes you. Guide him around the valley, but let me know what he says."

"Yes, of course. Do you think there is something wrong?"

"No. But we must be careful. I do not believe he had anything to do with Milton-ji's death, nor that he forced Milton-ji to show him the location of the valley, but many on the council do not share these feelings. We must be sure of him, so keep an ear on him."

"I am sure he is a good man."

Pita-ji let out a smile, but would never let Rani know it, so he said only, "Never be too sure of anything, but I pray you are right. Perhaps he can replace Milton-ji in our hearts."

"Yes, we all do" she said with a smile.

12 – Two Funerals

Raja did not know what to expect from the funeral. He remembered reading that in ancient India the wives were burned on the funeral pyre with their husbands. He was, therefore, quite relieved to see Anjali at the funeral. In fact, she was to light the pyre herself.

Milton was laying upon a bed in the center of the village "square" (for lack of a better word). There was a wood pyre build up around him. The people of India usually wear white at funerals, but as the people here could not see it was not unusual for them to be wearing the same clothes they had on before. The colors were drab, but mostly white as the sheep were doubtless white. Nevertheless, Raja deduced they must have a large number of black sheep, but there were black threads interwoven in some of the clothes, making them grayish in color from a distance. A few were almost black.

Raja did not want to disturb anyone, so he took a seat in the back and spoke to no one. Anjali was at the front mourning her husband, while many others gathered around. As Raja could not speak Hindi he was completely unaware of what was being said, but once Pita-ji had ceased speaking, Anjali arose with a torch in hand and moved toward her husband. She felt his forehead and kissed him. She then said some sort of prayer, or at least Raja assumed it was a prayer. After this, she stepped back and threw the torch under the bed. The kindle started almost immediately and very soon the entire pyre was aflame. Smoke filled the sunset sky.

Chanting of some kind continued for ten to fifteen minutes. Raja knew that no one could see him, so he figured there would be no harm in leaving. The fire was lit and his friend was gone. There was nothing he could do and he did not want to sit and chant when he did not even know what the words were which they were chanting. He took a stroll in the night air to clear his thoughts, but did not stray too far. He looked up into the smoke filled sky, and saw the streams of smoke heading up into the moon as if the moon itself were a vacuum sucking in the ashes of Milton.

There was much on Raja's mind. He was now alone. He had come here looking for something, although the truth is he did not himself know what that something was. His thoughts drifted from Rani to Milton and to the valley itself. It was truly beautiful. He began to think of Erasmus again and his proverb. "In the valley of the blind, the one-eyed man is king." Raja means king in Hindi. Raja could be a king, but he would be a good king. He had no ill intentions, but he felt his eyesight made him superior to these people. He considered them like lost children in need of a father. Yes, that was always in Raja's mind, and he had already tipped his hand to Rani. She knew that he claimed to have a fifth sense and many of the others had doubtless heard this as well. There was no sense pretending now. He would stick to his guns and show them that he did indeed have a fifth sense, and that he could help them, and lead them.

One thing which was constantly on Raja's mind was the fact that he would have to stay here if he was to be their king. A king cannot govern from a far away land. That was what held him back the most. He had been hesitant to give up his life of luxury (relatively speaking) in the United States for a small village, but Raja had no girl friend. He was never very good with women. He never knew what to say to women and his temper did not help. He had his share of women, of course, but no real love in his life. The women came and went like the wind, but something about Rani appealed to Raja. Perhaps it was her apparent innocence, or perhaps it was that mythical "love at first sight" which he had always scoffed at in the past. In either case, he wanted to make a good impression. If the people accepted him, then he would become their leader and show them a better way of life. If they rejected him, then he would return to the world outside with the discovery of a lifetime; one that would make him a famous explorer and professor ... or so he thought.

As Raja looked back he saw the crowd beginning to disperse. The funeral was over. He did not wish it to appear that he had not been there for the funeral of his own friend, so he quickly returned to offer his condolences to Anjali, and hopefully to speak to Rani again.

Naturally there was a line of people comforting Anjali, so Raja loitered around until the line had thinned somewhat. It was then he saw Rani walking up and speaking to Anjali. The line had thinned somewhat, so Raja thought that now was as good a time as any to speak to Anjali. He approached her and said, "I am sorry. He was a good friend."

"Yes. He was a good husband, and a man of Christ," replied Anjali.

Others came to speak to her, so he walked off with Rani, who asked him, "Why did you remain silent until now? Did you attend the funeral?"

"Of course I did." Raja was mildly offended by the question.

"Why didn't you say something to someone? We didn't know if you were here or not."

"I am sorry. I didn't see the need to bother anyone."

"See the need?"

"Yes, I didn't want to bother anyone."

"I hear," she said, which Raja deduced meant the same thing as "I see." Nevertheless, some young man standing behind them heard the remark by Raja and uttered a different response. He mumbled, "Didn't want to bother anyone? He is responsible for this."

Now Raja took this as a challenge. His temper flared up, and he turned to find the man. "Who said that!" He blindly pushed a elderly man out of the way while moving past him. There was one man and two women standing where he had heard the remark so he was fairly certain who had said it, and he again barked, "You have something to say to me!"

"Where have you been? You weren't by his side when he died and you weren't at the funeral. He said nothing about you before he died. Who are you?" The young man was visibly angry, but restrained. Raja, on the other hand, had trouble with restraint.

"What is that supposed to mean? Are you implying I had something to do with his death!"

"We are just saying that Milton-ji promised never to lead anyone here, and yet here you are and Milton-ji is no more."

With that remark Raja shoved the young man to the ground. He could not have been more than 19 years old, but Raja didn't care. He was furious, and while he may have had a right to be angry, the action did not sit well. Rani did not need to see to know what had just happened; nor did the others.

"Raja!" exclaimed Rani.

"Enough of this!" shouted Pita-ji who had witnessed the affair. He moved forward stretched out his hand to feel for the young man. As he attempted to get up, his shoulder hit Pita-ji's hand and he took hold of it. Pita-ji then assisted him to his feet.

"What is this bickering of the ashes of Milton-ji!"

"*Mujhe maaf kijye, Pita-ji,*" said the young man.

Raja did not understand the words, nor Pita-ji response, but it was softer in tone. The young man then walked off toward their stone carved homes. Pita-ji then turned toward where Raja was standing and in a calmer tone said simply, "The council would like to speak with you again tomorrow. We need to discuss what your role here shall be."

He did not wait for a reply, but immediately turned and walked away. Rani was still standing there, clearly disapproving of the events which had transpired. Raja finally said, "I think I will return to sleep again. Maybe I can catch up on my sleep tonight and I will feel better tomorrow."

"*Shub raatri.* Good night," she said.

"Good night."

*****

The sun had risen over the mountains a few hours before when Rani appeared at the doorway. She heard Raja doing something, and promptly asked, "Are you ready to meet with the council?"

Raja had been so busy he did not even notice her, but he was delighted to see her.

"Oh. Good morning. Yes. Just let me finish hanging this."

"What are you hanging?"

"A chandelier. I borrowed some incense candles from your priests last night and constructed this crude little chandelier."

Indeed it was. Raja had spent much of the night working on, before he fell asleep. He had taken six incense candles and fixed them to a dinner plate. Early this morning he had cut holes in the plate so he could then tie two ropes though the "four corners" of the circle. The hardest part was finding a way to fix it to the ceiling, since there was nothing there upon which to hang the chandelier. To solve this problem Raja had taken his climbing gear from his backpack and used the ice axes and picks. If they could cut into rocks, they could cut into the corners of the room. He then used the carabiner equipment to string a harness of sorts, and viola! He had a chandelier. Raja thought himself quite the genius inventor, but explaining this to Rani was not so easy as he had anticipated.

"What is a chandelier?"

"Well, it holds candles."

"Candles? You must be very religious to have that many incense candles."

Raja laughed. "Not in the least. The candles are so I can see at night."

"So you can 'see' at night?" Rani was very curious now.

"Yes." Raja finished his job, and now bent over to attach a carabiner to a small lantern he had made with one remaining incense candle. He then continued, "Candles give off light so I can see."

Rani simply shook her head, "Well we can discuss this later. The council is waiting."

Raja picked up the lantern and said, "I am ready. Let's go."

*****

It was daylight, but Raja remembered how dark it was in the council chamber. It was a rather large building and there was only the light from the door which had been blocked by bystanders trying to eavesdrop on the meeting. It is for that reason that he brought the lantern.

As he entered the chamber, he saw Pita-ji again seated in the middle. He now recognized Salah and Manish, as well as Jiven, the doctor. There were several others seated around in a circle, but Raja did not recognize any of them. He was actually relieved to see that the young man he had the altercation with last night was not among them.

"Come. *Baitho*. Sit," said Pita-ji.

"Thank you." This time Raja came and sat down without kicking anyone. He knew he had made a bad impression last time, so he was secretly proud of himself for thinking of the lantern.

"What is that?' inquired Manish.

"Sorry, what?"

"You set something down."

Raja forgot how sensitive the ears of the blind had become, not to mention that they could smell the incense candle. He had learned long ago that the four senses of the blind are heightened because they develop them more without eye sight to distract them. He had never even thought that they might hear him set down the lantern, although the smell of the candles was more obvious.

"Yes. This is my lantern." He paused for a second, but anticipating their next question, he added, "so I can see."

The men all began to shake their heads disapprovingly.

"Can you not find your way around yet?" asked Salah.

"I am fine when there is light."

The men appeared befuddled and mumbled to one another in Hindi. It was Jiven who spoke first, "Light?"

"Yes. When the sun is up I mean. The sun gives off light."

"Ahh, heat. You cannot see without heat?"

"No no. Heat is different. The sun gives off both heat and light."

Manish interjected, "So you can ..." he groped to find the correct word, "*see* when the sun is up, but not when it is down?"

*****

"Well, not as well."

"So what good is a fifth sense that doesn't work half the time?" asked Pita-ji.

"Well, I sleep at night anyway."

"So you only live half your life," remarked another.

"What? You sleep too."

"Yes," said Manish, "But we sleep when we need to, not because we are helpless at certain times."

Raja's temper was getting the better of him again, but he remained fairly calm, reminding himself that their ignorance was natural. "I am hardly helpless. I can do more than you, and I can do it better."

To this there was no answer; only dead silence.

"Why so silent?" The voice which broke the silence belonged to Rani, and startled Raja who thought she had remained outside the chamber.

"Oh, Rani. You startled me. I didn't see you there."

Several of the council members began to chuckle and all smiled, but they kept their mouths shut, keeping their thoughts to themselves. Finally, Pita-ji spoke.

"We called you here to see what your place in our society is to be. If you cannot find your way around, then it is obviously a problem we need to address."

"I can see fine. If it is dark I can bring my lantern."

"So you will have only one free hand with which to carry things?"

"Just what sort of work are you planning for me anyway?"

"Actually, that is what we wanted to ask you. What can you do?"

This livened Raja up a little, "Oh, well, I can show you a lot of things. I can show you the best places to plant your crops. I can design your buildings. There are many things I can do to lead ..." he caught himself at this point, since he knew they might not like the idea of a stranger "leading" them. He quickly continued, saying, "... to help you. My eyesight can assist you in many ways."

After a brief hushed silence, Manish spoke up, "Assuming you have this fifth sense you speak of, how can you help plant crops better?"

"Well, for one thing, if you plant your crops in the shade they will get no sunlight and they will not grow. I can see where the best place to get sunlight is."

Salah quickly retorted, "We can feel the heat of the sun. We know shade when we feel it. Is there something wrong with our crops?"

Puzzled expressions abounded. Raja was about to answer, but decided that he had offended them and kept silent.

Manish sensed this but pushed again, "And how can you help us design buildings when it appear you cannot even read."

"What?" a somewhat outraged Raja said, "Of course I can read!"

"Here then," Manish opens a book and pushes it forward, laying in nearby Raja, "this is a copy of the Bible your friend made for us. Please read any passage from the open page."

Raja quickly picked up the book without thinking, for anger interferes in normal brain related activity. He was about to start reading when he realized that the book was in some form of Braille. Greatly embarrassed, he finally said, "I can't read this. I can only read English."

This time it was Rani who answered, "That is English!"

"I mean ..." He ended his sentence here, not wanting to put his foot in his mouth any more. Raja was beginning to realize that he was doing far more harm than good. He underestimated how much these people could do without eyesight and he saw that he was offending them more than anything, so he dropped his shoulders in defeat.

It was now Pita-ji who stepped in to save Raja. "Perhaps now is not a good time. Our good friend has just passed away. Perhaps we should reconvene in a week. In the meantime, Rani will guide you around the valley so you can learn to adjust. Perhaps by next week you will no longer need your crutch."

"Crutch?"

"He means your ... lantern?" said Rani, struggling to find the correct word. In fact, Raja knew exactly what Pita-ji meant, but he wisely remained silent.

"Come. I will guide you around the village some more."

This pleased Raja, for he would at least get to spend time with Rani. Perhaps in a week's time he would know for sure what plan of action to take and how to convince the people of the valley that he did indeed have a fifth sense and could help lead them. In the meantime he felt as if he had just attended a second funeral in two days; his own.

After they left the Council Chamber, the council continued to debate Raja's place. Pita-ji spoke first.

"Perhaps he is just upset by Milton-ji's death. We have no reason to believe that he forced Milton-ji to come with him."

Manish seemed to like Raja the least of any of the council members. He said, "Perhaps, but I sense that even Milton did not entirely trust his friend. I feel that he brought him along because he was ill and could not make the journey alone."

Salah remarked, "Whether he was truly Milton-ji's friend or not, there is an arrogance in this one that I never sensed in Sir Milton. Milton was strange in his own way. That is natural as he was from a different culture, but I never sensed arrogance from him, and it is that which disturbs me."

Pita-ji now spoke, saying, "Yes, that is true, but as I said he may be distraught by his friend's death. Remember, Milton also used to claim to have this fifth sense."

"Do you believe there is such a thing?" asked Manish.

"If there is, it appears to be a weaker sense. He cannot 'see' when the sun is down. He stumbles inside buildings. He is like a child who is just learning to use his four senses and yet he is a full grown man. I do not understand this. How can they rely so much on such a weak sense? And as you say, his arrogance is the greater problem. He thinks himself superior to us, though he cannot even come to our meeting without a crutch."

He pauses to think and the rest of council remains silent in anticipation. Finally, he resumes, saying, "I suggest we keep an ear on him and hear what he does. Let Rani talk to him. She will be our ears. When we reconvene in a week we will wish to hear from Rani as well."

13 – Sight-Seeing for the Blind

Raja and Rani were walking side by side on Curry Street. Although the people could not see, they nevertheless cocked their heads toward him whenever he spoke or was near enough to hear. Raja felt as if the people viewed him as a phony psychic in a traveling circus. Why not? For all his talk of a fifth sense, he could not even do a simple thing like prove it existed! There were simple tests that might prove it, but he had already failed several because he did not think ahead. He had only looked the fool, and he knew it.

Raja kept going over it in his mind. He was a professor, but he was like an absent minded one. His emotions got the better of his brain. This was not uncommon, for despite all the Hollywood stereotypes, scientists are sometimes more emotional than the actors who portray them. They are humans, like all men. Raja was a smart man, but he was not acting like one. He had said he could read, which he obviously could, and yet he had not even stopped to think that blind men would use a form of Braille that he could not read. His pride intervened with his brain; a common thing indeed. He had a temper and a secret insecurity which he did not recognize. Yet others recognized it. Milton had seen this and even his students had seen it in his answers to students who dared to challenge him or who asked queries that he could not adequately answer. More importantly Rani saw it, but Raja could not. This is the irony of human nature. We shield ourselves more from our own mirror than from others. Milton had once said, "God cannot change us, until He breaks us. Don't make Him break you." Raja did not know it yet, but he was about to be broken.

As they were walking, Raja's mind was wandering. He was not used to chivalry simply out of habit, not disrespect, so he found himself walking ahead of Rani rather than waiting on her, for she was slow and steady in her walk, as one would expect from a blind woman. Rani, hearing him getting ahead and walking so briskly spoke up saying, "Slow down. You shouldn't walk off alone, you might stumble and hurt yourself. Even with our markers, you are still not familiar with the area."

Raja shook his head, but said nothing. She obviously did not understand that he could see. "So what are you going to show me today?"

"Show you?" she giggled a little, "You have funny words."

"What?"

"See, look, show, watch."

He only shook his head again, because he was slowly learning the wisdom of keeping one's mouth shut until the brain has had time to plot the words coming out of it.

"Why are you silent? Did I offend you?"

"No. Not at all. Shall we go."

"Yes, of course. It is just up ahead. It is a surprise."

A surprise, but Raja could now see the surprise. It was a beautiful flower garden. He thought to himself, "What good is a flower garden you cannot see?" yet he did not realize that he was speaking aloud, for Rani's hearing was very sensitive.

"What good is the wind? Or air? But you can't live without it. What good is a flower garden? What good is a heart that you can't see? Come, come."

Rani was clearly annoyed by his remark, but she then pondered how he knew about the flower garden in the first place, for she did not really believe in this fifth sense yet. "How did you know about the garden anyway? Can you smell them from here or did someone tell you?"

Raja rolled his eyes, "I can see them. Remember?"

Rani laughed a little, "Oh yes. I forgot."

It was obvious that she did not believe him, but Raja chose not to argue the point. "It is so beautiful here," he said.

"Yes, it is." Raja had a curious look at her response, until she finished her sentence. "I love the cool breeze and the smell of the flowers."

"You are beautiful too."

Rani smiled, but replied, "Thank you, but we have only met. How do you know I am beautiful?"

"I mean ..." he dropped off in mid-sentence.

"Yes?"

"If you could just see how beautiful you are."

"Thank you, but why do I have to see it?"

"If you could just see the things that I see, you would understand."

"If you could feel the things I feel you would understand."

Raja let out a little smile, and an even littler laugh. Rani detected this and it peaked her curiosity. She had heard about this 'sight' from Anjali. Milton had claimed to have this fifth sense as well, but to Rani it was like claiming to have a sixth sense would be to us. She didn't really believe it, but was curious about it. Finally, it was she who brought up the topic, to Raja's delight.

"Anjali told me about this 'sight' of yours, but she never quite understood it. Beauty to the eye, but it fades away so quickly. You 'see' my beauty, but will you when I am old? Will you still be able to see that beauty as you do now?"

Raja smiled and thought a little before answering. Finally he said simply, "Perhaps that is why our sight fades when we get older. So we can."

Rani didn't entirely understand the answer, but she knew it was clever somehow. Then Raja took her hand. She pulled back slightly at first, but more because of natural reaction than an aversion. She quickly relented and he held her hand.

"I can feel too, you know?"

The line did not have the anticipated response, for she said, "But does your sight affect your feelings? Anjali said it could."

"What?"

"Anjali said that Milton-ji's sight affected his other senses, especially feeling."

"Jim was a religious man. I am not."

"*Kya*?" By now Raja understood that this means, "what?"

"He believes in things which do not exist. That is blind faith."

"What is this word 'blind' you talk about so much? What does it mean?"

"Blind is when someone cannot see. If you believe in something you cannot see, that is blind faith."

"How do you know these things do not exist?"

"Maybe they do, but if I cannot see them, I have no reason to believe them."

"So what does gravity look like?"

"I don't want to fight," he said solemnly, "I am sorry if I offended you."

Rani paused and thought over some things which Anjali had told her. Finally, she pulled Raja close to the flower beds. Her feet felt the leaves which had been placed around the bed, so she knew where to step and not step. She then squatted down, still holding Raja's hand.

"Come. I want to 'show' ... is it? ... 'show' you something."

He kneeled next to her. "Yes?"

"Now close your eyes ... I am told that is what you 'see' with ..."

Interrupting he said, "of course. What else are eyes for?"

"Tear ducts of course. Not stop interrupting. I want you to close your eyes."

"Why?" he protested.

"No arguments," she shot back, but not in a mean spirited way, "Close them! Now!"

"Okay." He thought he would play along.

"Can you 'see' now?"

"No."

Rani put her hands on his face so she could feel his eyelids, but Raja opened them as soon as he felt her hands.

"Stop it now! Close them!"

He complied and her hands confirmed that they were indeed closed. She then reached down and plucked a tulip. She put the tulip in his hands, with one hand still on his eyelids.

"What is this?"

"A flower," he said.

She playfully slapped him, and said, "What kind of flower, silly?"

"I don't know, but it smells good."

"You don't know?"

"I don't know."

"Okay. Wait." She reached down and pulled another flower which she placed under his nose. "Surely you can recognize this flower?"

He inhaled its fragrance but had no idea what it was. "Is that a different flower?"

Rani now opened his hand, and replaced the old flower with the new one. She then clamped his hands down on the thorny flower.

"Ow!" protested Raja who immediately opened his eyes to see a rose, but he was more concerned with the thorn stuck in his hand.

"Now what?"

"A rose! Why did you do that?"

"So you can't smell, but it appears you can feel after all." She had a playful smile on her face and even in the tone of her voice, but Raja's was not so playful.

"Oh come on! What do I need to smell for when I can see?"

"You talk about beauty but you cannot even tell the difference in a rose and tulip without your

144

eyes. What beauty is there in something you cannot smell, or taste, ... or touch."

She waited for a response, but Raja remained silent, so she said, "You must learn that the most beautiful and precious things in life cannot be 'seen' or even touched for that matter. They can only be felt by the human heart."

He was only slightly angry, but that was not so much from the thorn as from her putting him in his place. He almost felt as if the ghost of Milton had come back to haunt him. Eyesight was such a simple thing to him. Why could they not understand it? He decided not to press the issue. She had won round one, but he would win the bout, so he reasoned.

"Come," said Rani, "I will guide you around the rest of the valley, but I want you to tell me what you hear, what you smell, and what you feel. Nothing else. You have to prove to the council that this fifth sense, if you really have one, does not handicap you. You must prove that you can live without it, or else it is nothing more than a crutch. Do you understand?"

"A crutch?" thought Raja. "A crutch?" Raja's thoughts did not make it to his lips. Instead he meekly replied, "Yes maam."

"Good. Come!"

Rani guided Raja to many things that day. She brought him atop a small plateau where he looked down upon the village, but she spoke of the wind at their backs, and the majesty of the open air. She took him to a lake and spoke of the sound of the rushing waters. She took him to a field of wild flowers and spoke of the smells of the flowers. And she took him to a crevasse where she spoke of the stillness of the valley and peace and serenity of the land. She told him that there were many other things she could guide him to in time, including a plateau that overlooks the whole valley, not just the village. All this "in time" she said.

It was already evening and the sun was setting. Rani did not need to be told this fact, for she felt the warmth of the sun dissipate and told Raja that it was time to return.

"I had a wonderful day, *mera sunder larki*." This is translated "my beautiful girl," for he was learning Hindi the best he could.

Rani smiled, "Thank you. I don't think I have ever heard anyone talk about beauty so much as you."

"But there is so much beauty to behold. So many things I cannot even describe to you. But of all these things you are the most beautiful of them all."

Rani was blushing now.

"You don't know what you are missing. The beauty of colors. The sight of a rainbow, or even the beauty of your own face."

"Is there also ugliness?"

"Not in you."

"That is not an answer. Tell me. *Bolo*."

"Yes. There is ugliness. But that only makes beauty all the more important."

"Why? I can feel beauty. I feel it all the time." She reaches out and touches his cheeks, "I can feel your beauty without having to ... 'see' ... it. Why do I need to see what I feel so strongly."

"Feelings are deceitful," he said with a strange bit of anger in his voice.

146

"And does your sight never deceive you?"

He hesitates, but concedes, "Yes, sometimes."

"And what about God? Can you see Him?"

"Oh, well I don't believe in Him."

"I know," she said in a disapproving voice.

"I don't believe in some big man in the sky guiding my destiny. I am the only one in charge of my life!" he replied with the sound of triumph in his voice.

"Oh really?" Raja could swear she was staring at him with those glazed white eyes. "Wait here." Rani went over and plucked a wild flower near the trail. She also picked up a small rock, but deliberately hid them in her closed fist. She then walked back over to Raja.

"Here. Choose."

Raja touched her left hand which she opened. It contained a rock. She then opened her right hand, containing the flower. "Would you like this too?"

"Yes, please," he said with a smile.

"Here," she handed him the flower, and dropped the rock. "Now tell me. Could you have chosen to take the flower if I had not offered it? Or would you have taken the rock?"

"What?"

"We claim to be masters of our own destiny, but the choices we make cannot be made unless they are offered first. You cannot choose something you have no access to. You cannot be the leader of a country, just because you want to be. You can only choose that which you are offered."

Raja looked into her eyes, but saw only the white glare. He thought for a moment that she knew of his desire to lead the people of the valley and took her comment personally. His eyebrow raised involuntarily, and he thought to himself that if she knows, then they might as well discuss it.

"And why shouldn't I lead? If I am capable of helping lead you people, why shouldn't I?"

Rani was rather surprised at what she perceived to be a change in topic, but the topic intrigued her as much as wondering *why* he had changed the topic so quickly.

"And why should you lead? Pita-ji has lead us for forty years."

"Because I can help. That is why. Why should tradition or nepotism rule out merit?"

Rani was intrigued. She thought to herself, "Who determines who has merit?" but kept silent. Milton-ji had spoken some about the politics of the outside world, and she vaguely remembered something about the growing popularity of "meritocracy" which he had insisted was just another word for a communistic dictatorship. Nevertheless, Rani did not allow her mind to drift too far for the subject. She chose to hear him out. "How can you help us?"

"Because I can see things you can't. I mean, don't get me wrong, you do much better than I would ever have thought, but what, for example, happens if wild animals attack? You can't even see to defend yourselves."

"There are no wild animals here. Unless you think the chickens and lambs are going to go wild."

"That is not the point."

"What is the point? You are a stranger here, remember?" Rani tried to hide her anger, but she was clearly annoyed by what she perceived to be arrogance. She just didn't understand that Raja, at least in his own mind, only sought to help them. Nevertheless, she was correct. He was new to the village and vowed to keep silent, for the time being.

*****

The next day Rani informed Raja that it was time to teach him how to work. If he was to be part of their society, then he would have to fit in somewhere. She would show him how they sustained themselves and how they lived. First she brought him to the goat farm where they get milk. Raja rolled his eyes, knowing they could not see him. "You want me to milk goats?" he pondered to himself.

Rani took Raja's hands and placed them on top of the goat, petting him and stroking him to show they were friends. Then he hands rolled down to the under belly of the goat to search for its utters. Raja, never conscious of just how much noise came out of his mouth when he would grimace or smirk, caught the attention of Rani. The sounds were barely perceivable to a sighted man, but acute to one with sensitive hearing.

"What is wrong?" she asked.

"Nothing. Why?"

"You are groaning like a goat with colic."

"A what ...? I was not," he protested in futility.

"Yes, you were. You sound like a growling *kutta*."

Raja laughed. He didn't know what a *kutta* was (it is a dog), but he realized now how the little things that we do not even notice were so much more noticeable to Rani. "I'm sorry, it is just that I am not a farmer."

"A farmer?"

"Yes." He was a bit puzzled but chalked it up to communication difficulties. "A farm. You know."

"Then how do you get food and milk?"

"I go to the supermarket, of course."

"Supermark...?" She was clearly unfamiliar with the word.

"Yes, you see. We go to a store where we buy the food."

"You buy it from your neighbor?"

"Well, sort of. It is imported from some other city or state or even country. Then we buy it."

"What happens if they don't send you any more food?"

"Well, of course they will. If one location quits for some reason, we just get it from another."

"So you don't actually support yourselves?"

"What do you mean by that?" Raja was naturally offended by the suggestion. "Of course we support ourselves."

"How?"

"How?"

"Yes, How? I just said that."

"We ... make the money that buys the products."

Rani stood there as if in shock, or perhaps deep thought. Clearly she did not understand. "You make money instead of produce?"

"Yes."

After a short pause, she just shook her head and said, "well here we make our own food and produce. Money is just for luxuries."

Raja knew it was going to be a long day. Indeed it was, but he didn't mind so much as long as he was with Rani. He had never really been in love before, but he felt as if he might be falling in love for the very first time. Often he would just stare at her like a school child, knowing that she could not see him and would not be offended, but his long moments of silence made her feel just the same. She would sometimes asks if everything was okay, to which he would assure her that it was so.

The next day was actual farming. Tomatoes and lettuce and various spices were cultivated. He learned how they had developed a system that would not require sight and allow them to work the farms very proficiently. He found himself amazed at how much they could do without sight, but every time he brought up the subject, he seemed to meet with skepticism or worse. They felt that his obsession with this fifth sense was driven by pride, so Raja would back off, but never completely.

The fourth day was poultry day apparently. Rani took him to the poultry farm where they gathered eggs, fed the chickens, and on rare occasions they would even kill a few of the older chickens for a grand meal. Many of the Hindus there were naturally vegetarians, but almost as many enjoyed meat on occasion.   Only beef is strictly forbidden except among the most devout Hindus. It was this day that Raja promised himself not to get into any arguments and he even tried to avoid discussing his sight. Instead he spent the entire day flirting with Rani, who politely kept him at arm's length so to speak. She also secretly liked the attention. It was a small village and most marriages were arranged, as is the custom in parts of India to this very day.

Contrary to many western stereotypes, marriage alliances were not merely for the rich, but often for the poor as well. There were many reasons that a parent might want to choose their son or daughter's mate, and those reasons are shared by most parents from western cultures as well. The reasons may vary for the noble desire to see a good spouse to more selfish reasons such as finances or prestige. In the case of the valley, there were not many suitors to start with. Raja estimated that this ancient civilization numbered about a hundred people, give or take twenty or thirty. The number of single men Rani's age were fortunately quite few, and this gave Raja an advantage. He never stopped to think, however, about her father. He did not even know who her father was, or if he was still alive. He did, however, notice the authority with which the village elder had over Rani and Raja had the distinct feeling that he did not like him. Although he would never admit it, Raja was actually nervous around Pita-ji.   He would not say "scared" but nervous. Something about him told Raja that Pita-ji neither trusted him nor liked him, but Raja liked Rani nevertheless.

As they were returning in the evening, Raja was in an unusually playful mood. He moved in front of Rani and walked backwards while flirting with her. She could tell from the sound and direction of his voice that he was doing just that and warned him to be careful.

"Step lightly and slowly. Even if you know the roads rocks or something may occasional fall from the cliffs and land in the road," she said.

"Well then I will jump over the rock!"

Rani was feeling a mixture of emotions. Like many women part of her liked the flirtation and attention, but part of her felt like he was embarrassing her and even mocking her. She promptly ignored him and attempted to walk around him, but he playfully continued to walk in front of her, regardless of which way she went. He was not paying attention to anything except the woman he liked.

"Come on. Tell me. Do you love me?" he asked in a playful manner.

"Love you? Please. You are sooo vain." She was not angry, but embarrassed. This embarrassment, however, soon changed hands as the man with eyes who was not watching where he was going soon tripped and fell over a gardener who was working by the edge of the road.

"Hear out!" shouted the gardener, who heard him coming, but he was not in time. Raja fell over him.

He picked himself up off the ground, laughing a little, and apologized, "I am sorry. I wasn't looking."

"Looking," said the angry man, "you are so insulting! Are you deaf too? Couldn't you hear me working here?"

Rani quickly intervened, "please Rupinder-ji, it is my fault. He was paying attention to me. Forgive us, please."

"Fine. It is the insult more than the action."

"Insult? I said sorry. Now get out of the way" Raja was now the angry one. His final words were muttered to himself, but aloud. "Blind fool."

"What did you say?" Rupinder too had exceptional hearing.

"Nothing," he began to walk off.

Rupinder turned to Rani and asked, "What is 'blind?'"

"I will tell you later. Please accept our apologies. He is still disturbed by Milton-ji's death." She then took off after him, where he was waiting a few dozen yards away.

"I am sorry," he said before she could say a word.

"You think we are fools?"

"No," he replied in a somber voice.

"You can't even walk or enter a room without falling down, and you think this 'sight' makes you superior."

He was in no mood to argue and said nothing in reply.

Rani, sensing this, finally said, "Just accept that this sight, whatever it is, is not worth separating us. And the others here will not take kindly to your superior attitude."

"Yes maam. I am sorry I ruined a perfect day. I really enjoyed our time together."

"Thank you. I will meet you again tomorrow, but remember this, Raja Sinha. The council will reconvene in a few days. Please do not antagonize them, and you would do best to forget your 'sight.' At least until we know you better, and trust you better. What ever joy you get from sight, enjoy it, but do not flaunt it on us. You will just anger the village ... and the elders."

Raja took this warning to heart. The events of the past week all happened so quickly it was hard for him to grasp. Many different emotions were flowing through him; fascination, pride, despair, fear, ambition, and even love. Sometimes he felt like Marco Polo or Columbus. Other times he felt like a phony psychic in a circus. These were the thoughts that passed through his head all night long. So preoccupied was he that he could not sleep most of the night. By dawn he had slept perhaps four hours.

*****

Almost a full week had passed. The council meeting was just a day away. Raja did not know what day it was, but he counted it as Saturday for Rani was taking him to their temple for religious services. It was a day of worship, although Raja worshipped no God, he did not seek to antagonize or offend Rani in any way. The temple was large and had simple non-ornamental columns. There were no idols, as Milton had told him, but the rest of the temple was similar to those he had seen in India, save that there was nothing ornate or pleasing to the eye. The aroma of candles, however, was quite strong and the chanting and singing echoed throughout the large chamber.

After looking around, Raja whispered to Rani while she was praying, "Where is Anjali? I don't see her?"

Several people nearby turned their ear toward him. "See her"? Raja instantly knew he had a mistake, but said nothing.

Rani whispered a reply, "She is a Christian. She meets with about a half dozen of Milton's converts in their own hut. Now please be quiet or pray."

Raja complied until the ceremony was complete, but as they were leaving he brought up the topic again. "How many Christians are there here?"

"Only about a half dozen. Most of us are Hindus. We were a little leery about his religion at first, but Milton-ji never gave us a reason to doubt his motives. Missionaries do not conquer; they teach and educate."

Raja laughed to himself.

"*Kya*? You don't agree?"

"I wouldn't call the Crusaders or Conquistadors teachers. That is all."

"And they were Missionaries?"

"Well, sort of."

"Sort of?" Rani knew better, but was trying to feel Raja out. Did he really not know the difference, or did he simply choose not to distinguish between them?

"Maybe they aren't, but I don't see the difference. Look at all the evil done in the name of religion."

She ignored the sight references, "see" and "look," which offended those nearby, and prodded him instead. "Evil?"

"Yes. Wars, torture, crimes, discrimination."

"And atheists don't do these things?"

"Well, no ..." he hesitated.

"Milton-ji told us about a man named Stalin and one named Mao-Tse Tung. And a few others. What were these men?"

"They may have been atheist," he reluctantly admitted, "but their crimes were politically motivated, not religiously motivated."

Rani's eyebrows raised up high, "and there were no political motivations for the Crusades or the Conquistadors?" She paused to wait for an answer, but when she heard none, she continued, "You talk about how many people die in the name of religion and yet men like Stalin, I am told, slaughtered over fifty million; many simply for the crime of believing in God. To blame religion for evil is like blaming property for theft."

Now Rani did not like to lecture, for this was not her style. Raja's silence said it all. Consequently, she backed down somewhat and finished by saying this, "Listen. Evil men are evil. I blame the men. If a religion teaches evil it is only because the ones who invented the religion are evil, but if a religion is true it is because it is from God. Religion neither makes man good nor evil, but only encourages one or the other, depending on its adherents and doctrines.

When you look at the great men of your history, they are almost always religious men. Our Gandhi, Mother Teresa, Moses, your Washington, Jesus."

"I guess Jim told you about them too, huh?"

"Yes, he was a good teacher and we all loved him."

"Me too." These were the last words he spoke on the subject, but Rani had one last.

"He taught us that the problem with mankind is not religion, but mankind. That is the problem which plagues mankind ... ourselves."

"Maybe he is right. Maybe that is why I feel like I want someone by my side. I don't want to live this life alone anymore. I want someone to be by my side." Those beautiful words not only touched Rani's heart, but was a sly way in which Raja changed the subject. Sometimes he could be so proud of himself.

*****

Raja spent the rest of the day sight-seeing, or in her case he thought maybe she was just hear-listening. In either case, he was about to retire for the big meeting tomorrow, when he saw Anjali standing out by the lake. He went over to greet her and talk to her. He had not actually had a chance to speak to Jim's wife in private. He thought this would be a great opportunity.

She was just standing there as if staring out into the lake, but she was being soothed by the sound of the wind on the lake. It made her feel calm and helped her think of Jim in heaven.

As he strode up, she did not move, but said, "Who is it?"

"Oh, I'm sorry. I was trying to be quiet," he said.

With a smile on her face, she answered him, while still facing the lake. "Hello. We have not had an opportunity to speak much."

"No, we haven't. I wanted to express my condolences. Jim was a good friend."

"I know. He spoke about you from time to time."

"Oh really," pleasantly surprised, "great. Some people here seem to think I was not his friend at all."

"Yes, I know. I have informed them that he did know you."

"May I ask what he said."

"Yes." She said nothing else, but neither smiled nor laughed.

"What did he say?"

"Oh, sorry," she laughs to herself. "I was in thought. I miss Jim so much."

"Yes, I understand."

She now turned to face him. "He said you two were magnets. Opposites attract, or that is what he said. He liked to be challenged, and even though you were always wrong, he enjoyed your conversations."

Raja smiled to himself, but could tell she was in no mood for a prolonged conversation. He was already tired and knew he had a big day tomorrow so he tried to conclude his remarks by saying, "It would be helpful if you could speak on my behalf tomorrow."

"I have already spoken to the council. That is why they know that you are a friend of his, but they also know the rest as well."

"The rest?"

"Let me give you some advice, as Jim's wife."

"Yes?" He was somewhat irritated now. He had always had a problem with temper and anger. It subsided as quickly as it arose, but it was a problem.

"I believe in this sight of yours. I could not have trusted my husband if I did not believe him, but this sight, whatever it is, is something the people here do not understand and people sometimes fear what they do not understand."

"Yes, I know." Raja was intrigued.

"If someone came up to you and claimed to have a sixth sense and then proved it by telling you all the personal details of your life, how would you react?"

He thought momentarily and answered honestly, "I would be angry. How did he know that? And why does he want to know about my personal life?"

"Exactly. We feel the same way. On our wedding night, Jim said he did not want to touch me until he had described my body. He felt this proved he could see. Of course, I half believed in his sight already, but we had agreed to keep it a secret. Nevertheless, now he wanted to make sure I believed him a hundred percent."

She paused in thought, reminiscing, and continued, "When Jim described my body in detail without having touched me, I actually felt violated. For a brief moment I was angry. He was my husband, and it was our wedding night, but that is how I felt. That is how you would feel if a man came up and described to you what he should not know about you and your secrets."

"I understand," he replied solemnly.

"Let me ask you something."

"What?"

"Why is it important to you that we believe in your sight? Is it pride or something else?"

"Pride?"

"Yes, pride. Why not just accept this gift as a gift from God and not try have us accept it, since we can never have it?"

Raja had never thought of it this way before, but he had a good answer nevertheless. "Because I can help you. You people have done very well here, but with a man who can see, you can do so much more. I just want to help."

The answer Anjali was about to give would make Raja very angry. He felt as if the people here could neither understand or appreciate what he offered them. He was half resigned to leave the valley and never return, but for Rani. She said just this:

"If a man came to your country and told you that he should lead you because he had a special power you do not possess, would your people let him? Or would they kill him? Jim said the later."

Furious at the remark, or perhaps at the implications of the remark, Raja said "good night" and turned to walk off. He was so angry he mumbled aloud his thoughts, completely unaware that Anjali was following a short distance behind him; only his thoughts consumed him.

"Those stupid fools. They don't know what I offer. 'In the valley of the blind, the one-eyed man is king?' Bah. 'In the valley of the blind, the one-eyed man is *God!* '"

14 – Judgment Day

Raja heard a clapping noise as he roused from his sleep. It was Rani's version of a door bell.

"Come on. Get ready. The meeting is in two hours."

Raja grumbled as he crawled out of the cot, but Rani was already gone. Judgment day was upon him. The day had come. He was relatively calm this morning; calm, but nervous. The reason is because he had come to a decision. If they did not accept him, he would return home, and he would asks Rani to come with him. In fact, he was secretly hoping for this, but he had serious doubts that Rani would want to come with him. They had, after all, only known each other about ten days. However, the promises of a new and fabulous world awaited her if she would come.

These were the thoughts that preoccupied Raja, but first things first. There was still a chance they would accept Raja and he could finally live up to his name (which means "king").

He went down to the lake to bathe. It was the custom there, but the women all bathed before the men awoke. Even though they couldn't see, the lake was still fairly crowded at times, so it was not appropriate for men and women to bathe at the same time and place. Raja had shaken off his desire to spy on Rani and the others bathing, although he had never really had the opportunity, given that he had been so exhausted this past week that he was never awake when the women were bathing, and they must have bathed before the sun rose, for the sun was just now dawning and it was the men's turn.

After cleaning himself and getting dressed, Raja waited for Rani outside his "hut," or cave. Raja chose to call it a "cut" from a stone cut cave hut, or simply "cut." He, for one, thought it was a clever title.

Rani walked up and heard his presence though Raja was all but *sure* he had made no sound.

"Shall we go?"

"Yes," he replied.

"First," she reached out and felt his arm. She then dropped her hand down his arm until she felt the lantern, which she grabbed.

"Just as I thought." She set the lantern down by the door. "I do not think the lantern will help your case. It is best to leave it here. I will guide you."

"Case? Am I on trial?" He noticed something grim in her voice.

"It may come to that. Your altercations were problem enough, but your latest comments are far more serious."

"My latest comments? Wha..."

Rani cut him off, "We don't have time. We don't want to be late. *Chello.*"

After a short walk they arrived at the council chambers. A crowd was already gathered around. It seemed as if the entire village was there.

"I cannot go in with you, but I will be in later to offer what little help I can."

Raja did not like the somber tone and replied only, "I see."

"And don't say words like that! It will make them think you are mad!"

*****

Raja entered the dark chamber and stood there. He was actually waiting for his eyes to adjust so that he would not make a spectacle of himself again, but it made him appear hesitant, which he was.

"Come," said Pita-ji in a commanding, but kind, voice.

Raja moved forward and those sitting around the circle made louder than normal noises, to insure that he could hear their presence. Some tapped the ground. Others cleared their throats. Such actions seemed a spectacle to the "observers," so to speak, standing outside. They were treating him like a child who was just learning to walk.

After Raja was seated, Pita-ji rose and spoke. "Members of the council. We are gathered here to determine what place, if any, this man has in our society and, if not, what we must do with him."

The address was short and formal, as he went on to explain the purposes of the proceedings. It was not apparent to Raja that he was, in essence, on trial. However, Pita-ji turned to address him directly following his short speech.

"Sinha-ji. You understand why you are here?"

"Yes," was all he could muster at this time, or at least all he chose to say. Perhaps it is best that he did not say what he was thinking, for "you

165

judgmental hypocrites! What right do you have to judge men" would probably not have helped his case.

"Do not be afraid, Sinha-ji. We are here to determine several things. First, we will give you a fair opportunity to prove that you have this fifth sense of which you speak." Raja perked up a little. "Second, we must address accusations made against you and determine your motives for being here and for wanting to be a part of our society."

"My motives?" thought Raja. "Who are they to judge my motives?"

"Finally, we will determine what to do with you, but have no fear. You will not be harmed in any way."

"Thank you," there was a touch of sarcasm in Raja's voice.

Pita-ji sat down, and Manish spoke.

"You say that you have a fifth sense."

"I do. It is called 'sight.' Would you like me to describe yourself?"

"Don't insult us, please. You could have heard about us from anyone by now. We have a fair and objective test, if you are willing to try."

"What is it?"

"We have drawn symbols on each of ten cards. We will hold the cards up and if you can get seven of the ten cards right, we will believe you."

"That seems fair. They are pictures and not words? Remember, I cannot read your Braille alphabet."

"Yes, we remembered. There are but small simple pictures and drawings on the cards. Things like Triangles."

"Oh, we used to do something similar back home." Raja was pleased.

"So is it agreed?" barked Pita-ji.

All agreed, and the first card was raised. It was quite dark in the chamber and Raja squinted to try to see. To his surprise the card did not appear to have anything written on it.

"Take your time," Manish said calmly.

"There is nothing written on that card. It is blank!" He thought they might test him by placing a few blank cards but the Manish simply laid the card down and picked up the second card.

"This one?"

It too appeared blank. Raja was beginning to think they were making a fool out of him. "There is nothing on that one either."

"You cannot 'see' anything?" asked Salah.

"Of course not. The cards are blank."

"None of the cards are blank." They saw no point in arguing about it. In their mind he clearly could not see. His protestations only made it seem as if he was mad. What Raja did not realize is that the cards had tiny bumps or impressions upon them. The blind cannot see so their alphabet and even their pictures were not drawn with lead or ink, but were impressions which could only be felt, and not clearly seen. The pictograms were a kind of Braille. Such a simple thing never occurred to either the village people nor to Raja, for we perceive the world through our own mind, and never that of others.

"This is irrelevant," said Pita-ji. "Whether you can 'see' or not, we have more important matters right now. You have had a week to get acquainted with our village and people, but we have heard some disturbing reports about you. We will give you a chance to respond to them."

"If it is about that Rupinder guy, I apologized. I admit I have a temper problem, but I have not harmed anyone. I just wasn't watching where I was going."

"And," Pita-ji seemed to be helping Raja to an extent, "you were upset over your friends death, so that might excuse your earlier altercation as well, but ..." The pause was dramatic. Raja thought very hard what else he had done wrong, but could remember nothing.

Finally, it was Salah who spoke. "Do you want to be our god?"

Raja's heart began to pound. A shiver went down his spine. He realized that his words the other night had been overheard. Those words were not easy to explain. He sat quietly, and once again felt anger consume him. This was clearly a trial, and he was the accused. This time, however, he tried his best to remain in control. He had already told himself that if they did not accept him, he would return home. It was now clear that they could not accept him.

"Do you have no answer?" asked Pita-ji.

"Gentlemen. It is clear that you neither trust me nor believe me. I could have helped lead you, but you fear what you do not know, so I will leave. You need not worry about me and you do not need to decide what 'place' I will have in your society. I will return home to my world, but I would ask a favor in the name of our mutual friend Jim Milton."

The council was taken aback, but very curious. "What is this favor?" asked Manish.

"Allow Rani, if she so chooses, to return with me. She can return to the valley someday, but let me show her my world as you have shown me yours. Let her come and discover the world outside your valley."

There was a hushed silence inside the chamber, but loud murmurs coming from outside. Soon Rani appeared at the chamber door. Pita-ji barked out some words in Hindi which Raja could not understand. Several more words were exchanged, and Rani entered the chamber.

"Rani, come sit. This concerns you."

Raja scooted over to make room for her to sit next to him, but she instead sat down at the northern end of the chamber. Again several words were exchanged in Hindi, which irritated Raja. He did not know what was being said, but he did not like it. After a minute of conversation, Pita-ji again spoke.

"Sinha-ji. I am afraid you do not understand the situation here. We cannot simply let you leave."

Once again a shiver went down his spine. They had promised that no harm would come to him and yet they were now saying he could not leave. How would they keep him there? What could they do to prevent him from leaving? He protested loudly.

"What right have you to judge me! I came here of my own free will to help you, and you dare to pass judgment on me? I do not recognize your authority to pass judgment upon me."

"Nevertheless, we cannot merely send you back to your world. We know full well the destruction that would befall us if the outside world were to know of us. Did not your friend Milton-ji tell you this? Did not our guardians in the monastery say as much?"

"Bah. Jim warned me about you too."

"So Milton-ji warned you about us did he? That is very interesting," said Manish.

Raja was furious. He was glad they could not see or they would surely have reacted, for he looked as if he was ready to kill them, but he was too angry to even speak. This was wise, for he had said far too much already. His fate was in their hands. Quickly many thoughts rushed through his head. If he left through the cave they could not follow. Surely the blind could not track down the sighted. No, he knew the threat was not from the village but from the monks above. If they saw him leave, they would hunt him down. Raja said no more. He was too busy formulating an escape plan in his mind. In the meantime, they had taken his silence for the right to remain silent.

Manish spoke, "Is there anyone who will speak for Sinha-ji?"

"Yes, I will speak for him." The words came from Rani, which was a refreshing surprise for Raja. He had thought she too had abandoned him. This little glimmer of light lifted his spirits ever so slightly.

"Speak," said Salah.

"Esteemed members of the council. I am indeed his only friend. Maybe I am more than that. But consider he is stranger in a strange land. Our customs are strange to him. He feels as persecuted as we do. I know he is immature and arrogant, but I feel a desire in him to do what is best. He wants to help us. Even if he is wrong, his motives are pure. Remember when Sir Milton first came here he too thought this 'sight' was unique. He was bewildered how we could do such simple things and we used to laugh at him. Remember? True, he did not have the temper that Sinha-ji has, but we all have our faults and sins. We all loved Jim. He brought us many things including the religion of Anjali and many others in our community. Even some of our laws have developed as a result of his teachings. If he trusted Sinha-ji, should we not trust him as well? If I trust him, will you not, father."

"Father!" She was speaking to Pita-ji! Raja felt a fool. Rani was his daughter! She was Anjali's little sister! He wasn't sure if this was a good thing or a bad thing, but he favored good, for her speech warmed Raja's heart. He felt that perhaps she did love him. He didn't really know, but having her on his side made his spirit calm. Perhaps she could influence her father.

Pita-ji now spoke in Hindi again, saying, "*Mere pyari beti, agar wo tumse pyar karta hai to wo yaha ruk jayega.*" He then turned to Raja and said, "I have promised no harm to you, and I will keep my word. There is nothing to fear. You are our guest. However, we must discuss what to do with you, and there is nothing more you can say to help your cause at this point. Preet will escort you to your hut where you shall await our decision."

A young man stepped forward, lightly clapping his hands. Raja stood up, looking at Rani all the time. He tried to read the expressions on the faces of the council members, but he could not. He could not even read Rani's, for he sensed something was different. Finally, Raja left with the young man named Preet, and the council resumed its discussion.

Said Salah, "I want to summarize what has been said in one way or another. This Sinha thinks because we cannot '*see*' we are stupid, yet he cannot hear or feel or sense like we can. He is like an infant in his four senses but thinks himself superior. This arrogance is compounded by the fact that he has no fear of God. You are his only defender Rani. What have you to say?"

She meekly replied, "Milton-ji trusted him."

Another member of the council, named Prakesh, said, "Did he? I sense that Milton-ji needed help to return to the valley. He was gravely ill. I do not sense that he fully trusted this Sinha, and I sense that neither should we."

"Please father," uttered Rani in a whispered voice.

Now Pita-ji spoke up with authority. "Gentlemen. We have a crisis here. Rani believes he can learn. I agree, but the problem is whether or not he *wants* to learn. If he attempts to return to the world outside he will surely reveal us and invaders will come to destroy our way of life. How can we prevent his leaving? How can we stop him? Can we afford to simply wait for him to learn?"

Manish responded first, "His arrogance is the greater problem. I sense it will prevent him from ever learning or accepting us. He has no fear of God and thinks us stupid if we do fear God. Such stubborn pride is most dangerous and intolerant."

"Please wise council members," pleaded Rani, "what can we do? If we cannot send him back then what can we do? We have promised no harm to him."

There was silence as each man was in deep thought. This was a situation that they had not faced before. No man spoke until Jiven broke the silence. He was not a man of words, but of science. The good doctor rarely spoke at meetings, or parties for the matter, but now he had something important to say.

"Good sirs. We have promised not to cause him harm, but we cannot simply let him leave. Of course it would be impossible for him to leave by way of the cave without provisions or help. Nevertheless, I fear he may try this anyway, and injure himself in the process. I base my belief on his actions and mindset. He truly believes in this fifth sense which seems to have a negative effect on his four true senses. Our eyes are tear ducts, but he thinks his eyes create some sort of magical fifth sense. I believe this is psychological. I believe I can cure this psychological mindset without causing any real harm. If it is a psychological malady, then we can cure it psychologically. A baby learns to walk because it must. Raja must learn to rely on his four senses, but we will need Rani's help to do this."

Rani did not even pause. She instantly replied, "Yes doctor. Tell us your plan."

*****

It seemed as if hours had passed. Raja was laying on his cot, as if a prisoner. He didn't know

173

what to expect, but he spent much of the time planning his escape and thinking of Rani. He would speak to Rani before making his escape whatever the decision of the council.

It was probably close to noon when he saw Rani enter. He sat up eagerly anticipating her comments. She was carrying lunch with her, which was a nice gesture, but Raja couldn't help but think, "Is this my last supper?" Was it a meal for the condemned man? Finally, he asked, "Well. What did they say? Am I to be boiled in oil? Flogged? Banished to the goat farm?"

Rani was almost in tears, "Do you trust me?"

"Yes, of course."

"Do you love me?"

The words were both welcomed and feared, for it said that the council's decision did not sit well with her if she was asking now for an affirmation of his love.

"Yes."

"Then please do not worry. Everything will be fine. And we can be together forever, if you truly wish it."

"What did they decide?"

"Here," she took a pitcher of water and filled a cup for Raja, handing it to him. "Drink this and we will talk."

Raja felt that Rani was softening him for some sort of blow. What had they decided? If he could live forever with Rani then the decision could not have been that bad, but he could see in her teared up frosty eyes that she was afraid. They had promised not to hurt him and Rani said they would be together, so what had they decided that made Rani so sad?

He drunk the water all the way down and even asked for more. He was thirsty, but he was also tired. It was the middle of the day and yet he felt like sleeping. Perhaps it was the events of the day, or even the past week. He had been unusually tired all week. As a professor he had been used to six or seven hours of sleep, which was less than recommended by doctors. Since the long journey down here, he had taken eight and even nine hours of sleep every night. It was his mind that was exhausting him. Many people, particularly world leaders, are not aware that the brain needs rest like every other organ in the body. When we actually use it, it gets tired, and Raja was very tired. He found himself drifting to sleep without even having heard the council's decision. He could only hear Rani softly saying, "everything will be all right. Everything will be all right."

*****

Many hours had passed, Raja did not know how long. He felt groggy. When he opened his eyes it was darker than usual. It must be night, but even the stars shone through the door at night. Instead it was pitch black.

"Rani??" Raja was becoming worried. He was unusually groggy and the darkness reminded him of the cave. Was he back in the cave? Had he already tried to make his escape and forgotten how he got here? He felt around, and touched his cot. He was still in bed. Now he was becoming more panicked. Something was terribly wrong.

"Rani!!!" He shouted. "Rani!!!!"

As he groped around, he ran into the wall and knocked over the cup he had been drinking from. He had been drugged! He knew it now. Rani had drugged him!

"Helpp!!!!"

As he fell to his knees he put his hands up over his eyes, but he could not see them. He could not even see his own hands pressed up against his face. It is then that he touched his face, and his eyelids. Horror struck him. His eyelids were sucked back and shriveled up in vacant bloody holes. They had removed his eyes.

15 – No Harm Done

Curses and screams could be heard coming from the cave hut. No one dared enter. Rani came running up, but hearing her footsteps and cries, several members of the community moved in front of her in a sort of reverse tackle move. She literally knocked them down as she tried to enter, but they held her back.

"Don't go in there. Who knows what he may do to you," they protested.

"Don't be ridiculous," she replied, and she pushed her way past them. Raja could hear them, but he could not see them.

"What did you do to me!"

Rani ran up and embraced him. He started instinctively to push her away, but instead clasp his hands to his face.

"What have you done to my eyes! You cut out my eyes!"

Rani simply kept muttering the exact same words over and over again, "It will be okay. It will be okay." This went on for some time as a crowd gathered outside the cave hut.

"You swore you would do me no harm! You all swore!!" he screamed.

"But everything is the same. We just removed your tear ducts," sobbed Rani.

"My tear ducts!! You stupid *kuttas*!" He still did not know what the word meant.

Pita-ji approached as he heard the cries, and asks the crowd, "Where is Rani? She didn't go in there did she?"

"Yes," said one, "but he has not harmed her. He is just screaming incoherently."

This Pita-ji could hear for himself, but he pressed forward to listen more closely. He could hear Rani whispering "It is okay, my dear. It will be all right," over and over again. Pita-ji then turned to the crowd and ordered them to disperse. He himself remained at the doorway, ready to charge in should Rani cry out for help, but no cry was forthcoming from her. Only the cries of Raja.

After ten to fifteen minutes of rage, Raja got up and tried to make it to the door. He stumbled and fell several times, crashed into walls, which he promptly pounded with his fist, until they bled.

Rani kept trying to embrace him, and hold back his pounding fist. "You are bleeding. Please let me help you."

"You have helped me enough!"

Finally, he managed to storm out the door, and run off into the distance, stumbling several times, but each stumble was just an expression of rage for him. He didn't care. Pita-ji, moved up behind Rani who was following behind him and took hold of her.

"Let him be, my daughter. Let him be."

"But he will hurt himself," she sobbed.

"He wants to hurt someone right now. It is best to let him vent his rage on the rocks and trees and stone cliffs, than to vent it on you."

"Oh father," she began to cry on his shoulders. "He knows I gave him the sedative! I was responsible. I was!"

Rani couldn't stop crying so he consoled her by saying, "No dear. I was responsible. I admit that I am sometimes harsh and unfeeling. It is my job to protect this Valley and its people, and I have sometimes forgotten what it means to be human.

"Give him time, Rani. If he is worthy of your love, he will forgive. If he is not, then nothing will change him. Just do the best you can, and leave the rest to God."

Off in the distance they could still hear him screaming at the world and at them. They even heard the splash of water as if he was trying to drown himself, but they knew he was simply out of control and in a rage. The water would cool him down.

*****

Pita-ji urged everyone to avoid him for several days until he had calmed down, unless he first called out to them. Even then they were not to speak to him without someone else present. Neither Pita-ji nor Jiven, nor anyone else had expected this level of rage from him, and many of them were scared. They had done no harm to him. It was nothing more than like having your wisdom teeth removed or having an appendectomy. Only Anjali and Rani understood. Anjali understood because she came to believe in Milton's sight. She was not present when the decision was made by the council, or she would have fought against it. Rani understood only after the surgery. Now even Pita-ji was beginning to wonder whether or not he had made a mistake.

"How is he?" asked Pita-ji.

"Oh father, it has been three days and he has not even left the hut."

Rani had been crying all these days. She entered the cave hut to give him his dinner these past few days, but Raja would always ask, "Is it poisoned this time?" He was subject to constant mood swings. He literally did not know how to do anything without his eyes. Even going to the bathroom (or mother nature, as they had no bathrooms) was a struggle for him. Was he watering someone's lawn he would wonder. Frankly, he didn't much care. Sometimes he deliberately watered the flower garden for them as a sign of contempt, but the gardeners knew he was coming and stayed out of his way, so there was no harm done. Everyone pretty much stayed out of his way except for Rani and Anjali, who had once approached him. It was her, perhaps, that helped to calm his rage, if only a little.

Anjali had explained to him that she would have told them not to do it, had she known. She told him that they did not believe they were harming him. She explained Jiven's theory, which only made Raja more angry at their stupidity. In the end Anjali had feared she had done more harm than good, but in reality it was she who had convinced Raja that they were guilty only of gross ignorance, and not of spiteful vengeance.

One day Pita-ji made the simple observation, "He seems to be taking this rather hard."

To this Rani responded, "Yes father. His fifth sense was real. At least to him. Didn't Milton-ji also claim to have had a fifth sense?"

"Perhaps so, but we had to protect ourselves. We could not trust him, and Milton himself warned us of the outside world as have the monks. It is an evil world and we must protect ourselves from it."

"Oh father, are we any better? Are we any different? He looks down on us because we do not have this 'sight' and we look down on him because he does. How are we any better or different?"

Pita-ji felt sympathy, but he was a hardened leader, so he replied, "We all have to make hard decisions, but we have survived and thrived for thirty-seven generations without this 'sight'. He can too. When he gets over his self pity, he will learn to live like the rest of us. Just give him more time."

Sobbing, she said, "but I don't know if he will ever forgive me."

"It was not your choice. He can't blame you. It was me who made the ultimate decision. Let him hate me if he must."

Rani embraced her father and cried some more. Pita-ji was beginning to worry that she needed to drink more water or she would surely dehydrate for her tears had scarcely ceased, whereas Raja could no longer cry at all.

"Go, my darling. See if he needs anything."

"But last time he screamed at me and threw a cup at me!"

"He is angry. He needs you. Trust me. He needs you."

Rani wiped away the tears and went to get some water to bring him. It would be a nice gesture, although she could already hear his sarcastic remarks in her head. "More drugs?" he would say to her.

As she entered the cave hut, she tried to speak without her voice breaking. "Raja, dear. I brought you some water."

There was no answer. Was he giving her the silent treatment? Surely he had not left or someone would have heard him. Perhaps he was sleeping.

"Raja?"

She advanced slowly into the hut. "I brought you some water."

Again there was no answer.

"Please don't be angry with me. We never intended to harm you."

As she advanced toward the cot to see if he was perhaps asleep, she slipped on something wet. She thought it might have been some water he had thrown at her earlier, but there was far too much of it. She reached down to feel it, and it was far too think to be water. As she raised her hands to her nose to smell it, a chill went down her spine. It was blood!

"*Bacchaoo*!!! *Bacchaoo*!!!" she screamed, which means "help!"

She quickly crawled over the cot and found Raja there bleeding and unconscious. "*Jiven ko bulao!! Jaldi! Jaldi!!*"

16 – Making a New Life

The whole village was roused. Raja had tried to commit suicide. Rani had been in a panic, but Anjali came and prayed with her. Indeed, the whole village prayed, but Anjali met in private with Rani and the few Christians who resided there while the rest of the community offered incense at the temple. Jiven, however, spent all his time with his patient. They did not have the ability to do blood transfusions, so the blood had to be restored naturally. Raja would live, but he was very very weak and would be bedridden until his body naturally replenished his blood cells.

During these few weeks, Raja was too weak and too tired to yell at Rani. She was secretly glad of this for it gave them a chance to talk, and for her to constantly plead his forgiveness until he was so sick of her pleas that he never again brought up the subject of her having drugged him. The rest of the village, however, Raja would not so easily forgive.

Rani became the self-appointed guardian and teacher for Raja. He would have to learn how to survive without his eye-sight, and someone had to teach him. It would be harder than it was training a child who had never seen, for Raja, after thirty plus years, was so accustomed to his eye-sight that his other senses were deadened. He did not know how to navigate the world without sight. Children learned somewhat instinctively, but this adult had to be taught step by step, and it would take great love, and great patience, to do this, for Raja was not a particularly sociable person when he could see, and now he knew only anger and emptiness.

His heart was void and felt like a vacuum. He was lost with no sense of direction in his life. Like many in this world, he longed for a purpose in life, but every man fills this empty void in his life one of several ways. Some fill the void with money. Some with fame. Some with power. Some with sexual conquest (a variant of power). Some fill it with man made religions, but it can only truly be filled by God. Blaise Pascal, the famous scientist of the seventeenth century, said in his work *Pensees*, "[man] tries in vain to fill [this void] with everything around him ... though none can help, since this infinite abyss can be filled only with an infinite and immutable object; in other words by God himself." This quotation has often been paraphrased and circulated as "there is a God-shaped vacuum in the heart of every man which cannot be filled by any created thing, but only by God."

In the past Raja had succeeded in filling this void, or so he thought, by preoccupation with one thing or another. Now he could not. All seemed lost. He knew he could now never escape the valley, and even if he had, he could not envision a life like he once had. He had become so desolate that he had tried to kill himself, believing that there is nothing beyond death. How great the despair of the agnostic! Not only was his life meaningless, but so also his death, but for those who fear God death can give meaning to life, when we serve God and our fellow man.

Indeed, some of the great men of history were unknown until after their death. Great literature is often unknown and unappreciated during the author's lifetime. The same is true of many great artists and even scientists. Gregor Mendel, for example, was a simple monk who tended his garden and performed scientific tests on cross breeding. After his death, other scientists discovered his work which became the basis for modern genetics, and a thorn in the side of every Darwinists ever since.

*****

It had been seventeen days since his suicide attempt. He had been allowed to get up and walk around, but this was only for exercise. He had no idea how to get around and had to be supervised even for his exercises. Today, however, Rani had gained permission from Jiven to take Raja out and start showing him (forgive the terminology) how to survive in a world without sight. She had leave to skip her normal work duties and devote herself to Sinha-Ji's education.

Rani was waiting for Raja to wake up and standing outside his stone hut. Pita-ji walked up and after greeting one another, he recognized Rani's voice and spoke to her.

"I hear you two are getting along now."

"Yes, father. I think he has forgiven me, but I still don't think you should talk to him just yet."

"Yes. I know we were brash and perhaps a little harsh, but fear does that to people. We had to protect ourselves and it seemed the best way for him to remain here with us and no longer be a threat."

"I understand, but I feel he has lost something you and I can only imagine. Perhaps that is why we cannot understand his pain. And perhaps that is why we feared him."

"True. My little daughter is becoming wise in her old age."

"Old age!" Rani feigned righteous indignation.

"But you are right. We all perceive people through our own minds. We conform people to our perceptions. It is hard to understand people outside of ourselves, because we have no other perspective from which to consider them, or 'see' them as your Raja would say."

"But when we know God we can view things a little differently, can't we? After all, He is the only one that knows each of us inside and out."

"Indeed. Does your Raja believe in God now?"

"I don't know. He is very different from Milton-ji."

Reminiscing, Pita-ji said, "Yes. I remember I used to argue with Milton about his one God and our gods. One thing he said that we both agreed upon was 'if you will just pray that the true God will reveal Himself to you, you will have your answer sooner or later. God hears all who call upon Him, no matter where they come from, no matter what have believed, and no matter what they have done. God is not deaf.'"

"No, God is not deaf," she smiles to herself a little, "but sometimes I wonder if He is a little blind."

Pita-ji laughed and left Rani to Raja who had heard the talking outside his hut. Rani wondered just how much he had heard, but she never asked him and he never told.

"Where are we going?" he asked.

"I am not going to tell you. That is your first test. You have to tell me when we get there."

Raja wanted so badly to rolls his eyes, but he had none so he continued to follow Rani closely. As he walked he had followed the sound of Rani's voice, but paid no heed to what he was walking upon. When Rani took a right turn at Onion Street, she neglected to tell Raja that they were turning right. He heard the sound of her voice, but was several steps behind, so he veered off the right, not conscious of the fact that he had stepped on leaves, which represented a "warning track" to indicate the edge of the road. In short, he had cut the corner too sharply and tripped over the small pebble edge of a garden, falling flat on his face.

"Raja!" she heard the thud and cried out, "Are you okay?"

An embarrassed and unsettled Raja replied, "Yes. I am fine. But why would anyone put stones in the road!"

"First of all, you were not on the road. Remember to feel what you are walking on. The leaves indicate the roads edge. Secondly, walk lightly. You are trampling around like an elephant," she began to laugh.

"Very funny," but he was not laughing. He brushed off the dirt from his clothes and tried to get back on the road, kicking up some more pebbles in the process.

"Remember, if you step lightly you will not fall every time you hit some pebble or rock in the road. If you are tramping around like an elephant you will fall on your head every time, and I don't want you to hurt your little stubborn head."

There was a playfulness in her voice, but Raja did not appreciate it at all. He was being treated like a child and he knew it. Nevertheless, he took the lesson to heart. He was a child in a way. Even worse, for a child learns without any preconceived notions. Raja had thirty some years of preconceived notions to overcome, and he was finally starting to realize it.

Having sensed his frustration, Rani took hold of Raja's arm, which, to her surprise, he did not pull back. "This way. Step lightly."

After maybe twenty or thirty more yards, Raja was not good at counting steps, they stopped.

"Now here, feel the leaves under your feet?"

"Yes, a warning track."

"Very good," she said with a smile. "Now gently feel for the border with your feet."

Raja promptly kicked a small pebble wall, about three to four inches tall.

"No. Gently I said. Gently. Someone will have to repair these borders now." After brief silence she reassured him, "It is okay. Just feel around with your foot gently. You should be able to do it the same way you used to do with your hands."

He said nothing, but swished his feet around, knocking over a few more pebble border walls.

"Okay, that is enough. Now step over gently, and then wait for me."

She stood back to see if he could successfully perform such a simple task, and he did, but not without causing some more damage to the pebble border wall. Rani shook her head, realizing that it was not going to be an easy task, but kept quiet. She decided positive reinforcement would be best.

"Very good, now wait." She stepped over the wall as if she could see it. "Here, now kneel down."

They knelt down, and Rani plucked a flower from the flower bed. "Where are we?" she asked.

"I don't know."

"Well, do you smell anything?"

He inhaled but could not recognize the smell. Rani then raised the flower to his nose. "How about now?"

"Ahhh, it is a flower. We are in the flower bed."

"Verrrryy good," she said with a broad smile, "now tell me what kind of flower."

"What kind?"

"Yes, what kind."

They had done this before. Raja remembered the encounter, and he remembered that he knew nothing about flowers, but he played along.

"A rose?"

"No. Try again."

"A ..." Raja did not even know the names of most flowers, so he was hazarding a guess, "wild flower."

He felt a light playful slap on his hand, "No! Here. Take it and wait here."

He took hold of the flower, and her hand. She did not immediately pull it away, but used her other hand to gently remove his. She was speaking to him with her hands. This was something Raja did understand. She did not withdraw her hand because she secretly liked him, but she was a proper woman and not to be taken lightly. This body language spoke louder than any words.

Rani got up and moved off, but he could tell she had not gone far. She was picking more flowers. When he started to stand up, she could hear him shuffling and said, "No wait. Stay there. I don't want you trampling the garden!"

He sat back down, smelling the flower in his hand. He then heard her sit back down close to him.

"You are holding a tulip. Now smell it."

He inhaled as if snorting some probably illegal substance.

"Don't snort it! Smell it. Softly. You must learn to take things slowly, softly, gently. You do everything fast, hard, and carelessly."

"Yes, I know. It is the hustle and bustle of my world. We never stopped to smell the roses," he chuckled a little.

She did not understand the joke, but smiled anyway. "Now here," she handed him another flower. "This one is a daffodil."

He gently inhaled its fragrance, and then inhaled the tulip again. "Are you sure there is a difference?"

"Are you joking, dear?"

He said nothing, but inhaled each one again. "I think I see."

"You see? I thought your eyes were your sight source?"

Raja didn't know whether to be angry or to laugh. "It is a saying. It means I understand."

"Sorry, Sinha-ji. Why do all of your idioms involve sight?"

"It is the most dominant of our senses."

"Is that why you can't do anything without them?"

He did not appreciate the innuendo, but it was true enough. He couldn't even get around without her help, and he knew it. "Yea. I guess so. I just never noticed before. I can tell you what a rose looks like and I can tell you what a tulip looks like, but I could not tell you what they smelled like."

"Why? Did your fifth sense blind you to all your other senses?"

"In a way it does. We used to say 'seeing is believing' and yet the eyes deceive in so many things ..." he pauses in reflect, and then added, "particularly with Photo shop."

Raja started to laugh, but she did not know why. Other onlisteners cocked their heads, wondering what joke they had missed.

"I don't understand."

"Never mind. I guess I just had to see things to believe them, but when I stop to think about, there were a great many things in science that I never actually *saw* but I *knew* they existed because the evidence was undeniable. Gravity, for example. Such a simple thing, but we don't actually *see* gravity, we merely see its consequences. It has no chemical formula nor atomic weight. We didn't need a microscope to know what oxygen was and yet it keeps us living. I guess, that is what Milton was always trying to tell me all those years."

There was a pause in which he was reflecting, broken by Rani's voice. "Here, one last flower. Try this one."

He reached out to grab the flower when he was stuck by a sharp thorn.

"Ow! That is a rose!"

"You *are* getting better," she began to laugh.

"That is the second time!" he protested. Indeed, they had tried this earlier when he had sight, but only now was it beginning to sink into his brain. He spend a few moments smelling the flowers and trying to memorize which was which. He also stroked his hands over the pedals of the flowers. After thirty some odd years, Raja had learned the difference in a tulip and a daffodil.

"Come, I want you to feel something else."

Raja kept his sarcastic thoughts to himself and followed, only tripping thrice. He was actually quite proud of himself. Rani, for her part, intentionally did not help him. He had to learn for himself. If he fell, he would have to get back up, just as children do.

After traveling what felt like a mile (it was, in fact, only three-quarters of a mile) Raja could clearly hear a water fall. His ears were not so insensitive as to miss this. She was taking him to a waterfall, and he wanted to make sure she knew that he knew.

"It is a waterfall!" he said proudly.

She giggled a little, for he apparently believed that stating the obvious was a victory. "Veryyy good, but I want you to feel something. I want you to feel the water."

"Feel the water?" he was clearly disappointed. "Here, kneel down."

He did so when he felt a splash of water in his face and heard a laugh as Rani turned and ran off a few yards, still laughing. Raja tried to follow her, but stumbled into her. She wasn't sure whether it was really an accident, or play, but she laughed along with him. Their hands met and embraced.

"Why is it so cold all the sudden?" Raja's words may not have come at the opportune time, but he did shiver from the cold as the wind was blowing a chill across the lake.

"Because it is night time. The sun has gone down."

"How can you tell?"

"Here," she lifted Raja's hands in the air, and turned his palms upwards. "Can you feel that?"

"What?"

"Nothing?"

"No, what am I feeling?"

"Nothing!" She taps her fingers on his palms. "If it were daylight, you would feel the sun beating down on your palm."

Raja did not fully understand. What if it was cloudy? Perhaps it was a her inner clock combined with the cold and the lack of feeling the sun's heat. In this he was not entirely wrong.

"Will I see you in the morning?" he asked.

Giggling somewhat, she said, "No, but I will be here. Okay?"

"You had better be. You are all I have now."

She gripped his hands again and pulled them to her heart, "Can you feel that?"

"What?"

"My heart?"

Smiling, he replied, "Seriously?"

"My dear Raja, you see with your eyes. We see with our hearts."

17 – Acceptance

Three months had passed. Rani and Raja were at their favorite hideaway. It was a cave behind the waterfall. They liked the feel of the cave and the silence therein. The waterfall could be heard but softly as a gentle massaging. They could feel its beauty and hear the silence, or to be honest, they could hear the little noises to which we do not even pay attention. The sound of rushing waters, the sound of the wind, and sometimes even the beat of their hearts. What they could not see were the hundreds of fireflies which illuminated the cave. There was so much beauty around. Beauty to the eye. Beauty to the ear. Beauty to the senses. But we never acknowledge all the beauties. We only pay heed to one or two, and the beauty of the trees is lost among the forest.

"It is so quiet here," Raja pondered aloud.

"Quiet?" replied a surprised Rani, "You can't hear the waterfall outside? Listen carefully."

"I know. I hear it. That is what I meant."

Rani was now even more confused. "You are a strange man Raja Sinha."

He began to laugh out loud, and then explained, "The world I came from was what they called a 'concrete jungle.' Stone, mortar, rocks, iron, and steel. Noise was everywhere, and the beauty of nature nowhere. To me, this is quiet and peaceful."

"Oh," she thought she was beginning to understand. "Is that why you learned not to use your other senses?"

Again Raja laughed. "Maybe so. Maybe so."

"But if there was so much ugliness, as well as beauty, why did you rely on your sight so much?"

"Maybe because there is so much beauty to see as well. So many things I cannot even describe to you." He paused to reflect and to take in the peace. "It seems so serene here. I wish I could see it."

Now Rani was slightly annoyed again, "Why do you always wish for what you don't have?"

"What? I can't wish for what I do have."

"Of course you can. You can wish to appreciate what you have."

There was silence from Raja, so Rani continued, "Didn't you say earlier that you lived in a jungle of stone, or something like that?"

"Yes. A concrete jungle, it is called."

"Well. You said it was noisy and there was no beauty to be seen. Right?"

"Yea?"

"And yet you miss it. You miss what you had because you never appreciated what you had. You want what you don't have, and when you have it, you forget it."

"Is everyone here a philosopher?" he thought aloud.

"Am I a good one?"

Now smiling, he answered, "You are good. You are very good."

She giggled and then crept over to a pool of water in the cave. She bent down to drink, and invited Raja to join her while she washed her face in the cool water.

As Raja made his way over the pool, he tripped over a rock.

"You still haven't learned to step lightly, have you?"

She extended her hand out to him. Once he felt her hand, he moved next to her and squatted down.

"Are you okay," she asked.

"I am fine."

"I am sorry. It is very rocky in here. You need to step very lightly. I should have told you."

"No. You are right. I must learn on my own."

"Come, drink some water. We call it *pani*."

As Raja drank some water and washed his face, Rani took a small fruit out of her sari and held it out over the pool.

"Where are my little cave birds?" she said.

"What is a cave bird?"

At first oblivious to his question, she called out to the cave birds. "Here you go my little friends." Then, with her hands still extended, she spoke to Raja, "I believe Milton-ji called them cats ... or was it bats?"

"Bats?"

Suddenly a little bat landed on Rani's hand began to eat the fruit.

"Be careful? They might bite you, or suck your blood," he warned.

Rani began to laugh, scaring off the little creature. "Where do you get these ideas?"

"Well fruit bat or vampire bat, they still make my skin crawl."

"Come back, little cave bird. Come back." She again turned to Raja, "But why? They are soft."

Another bat landed upon her hand and began to feed. She stroked it, and it did not flee for they were accustomed to her feeding.

"Here. Feel."

Raja felt up her arm to her hand, but just as he touched the bat, it flew away.

"Sorry."

"It is okay. It takes time for them to become accustomed to people."

"Are you sure? Do they know you are feeding them? They can't see you know?"

"What?" she was somewhat aghast. Was he on about *that* again?

"Yes. Bats are incredible creatures really. They are blind but they know where everything is even in mid-flight. They use sonar, you know? Amazing really."

She wasn't sure whether to be mad or just laugh, but a giggle did emerge before she responded, "I don't know what sonar is, but why wouldn't they be able to get around and know where everything is? You are a mystery Raja."

He knew he had somehow offended her and decided not to explain the intricacies of radar and sonar. Instead he drifted off again into another mood swing. A solemn Raja now spoke saying, "Rani. I want you to know. Even though I am still angry, very angry, I don't blame you. Ever since I saw you and your beauty, I fell ..." he stopped, not wanting say the dreaded "love" word.

"You fell?"

He laughed at himself, "Yes. I fell."

Teasingly, she asked, "Is that normal?"

"Only when someone is as beautiful as you?

"But how could you tell I was beautiful? You didn't even know me?"

He started to laugh out loud.

"What?" asked Rani.

"You don't know what you missing. The beauty of colors. The sight of a rainbow, or even the beauty of your own face."

"What is a rainbow?"

"Oh, it is beautiful. You see all the different colors shining through the water vapor in the air."

"Colors? You mentioned that once before. What are colors?"

"I wish I could explain. Think of it as like a texture. Every color is a different texture."

"So color is a texture?"

"No. That is just an analogy. You can't feel it, you can only see it."

Clearly Rani was disappointed, so he felt further explanation might help.

"The sun gives off heat. Right?"

"Yes."

"Well, it also gives off something called ultraviolet light which cannot be seen by the human eye unless it reflects off a surface."

"I thought you said it was something you see."

"Yes, but only when it is reflected off of a surface. You can't actually see the light unless you see it reflected off of something."

"So you can't see it, unless you see it on someone else?"

"Yes," smiling with a small bit of triumph.

"Ohhhh, like God!"

Raja's triumph turned to failure as he could only say, "Oh, God. Well, ... yes. Sort of." The last few words were barely audible.

Rani giggled a little. "Oh, I forgot. You don't believe in God."

"Well, not really."

"Because you can't see Him?"

Raja was curiously silent. He used to argue more, but was more and more quiet these days when it came to religious debate. He convinced himself that it was out of courtesy, but that had never stopped him before. No, he knew His arguments fell flat in a valley of the blind. They could not see colors anymore than he could see gravity. In fact, one might dare say that his eyes were being opened for the first time. Logic demands more than meets the eyes. Faith is not believing in the impossible, but trusting in the unseen. One has faith in friends. One has faith in himself. One has faith in God. Faith is part of every man's life; even Raja's. He was beginning to have faith in Rani, although it was her who had drugged him. Yes, it was her who was responsible for all his misery, and yet he was slowly coming to have faith in her.

"Sight must be something special. I can only imagine," she conceded.

"Yes. So many beautiful things to see. Rainbows, sunsets, fields of flowers, ... even eclipses."

"Eclipse? What is that?"

"It is when the moon blocks out the sun, and there is no light until the moon passes. It is truly beautiful." He thought for a moment and then added, "There is actually supposed to be an eclipse in a couple of days. At least I think it is a couple of days. I have forgotten the days lately, but I am pretty sure it will fall two days from now. I like astronomy, you see."

"No, I don't."

"I mean ..." he was half apologetic, realizing our common sayings were either offensive or made no sense, but she did not really mind anymore. She thought he talked funny, like a man with a unique accent.

"Don't worry. I would like to feel this eclipse if possible."

"You can't feel it. You can only see it."

"Really?"

Raja says nothing else. The memory of seeing an eclipse reminded him again of what he had lost and he slipped in a depression. These mood swings are common for those who have experienced deep loss. One moment he is happy and forgets his problems, but another moment even a tiny thing can remind him of his loss and he becomes depressed. Rani was aware of this, and thought of a way to change the topic.

"Do you want to go back home?"

"Home?" he said somewhat mockingly, "Yes. I want to go back home ... but I can't."

Rani felt sad now, "I meant ..." Her voice dropped off into oblivion for she had no idea what to say. Finally, she thought of something that might cheer him up.

"Come with me. I want to introduce you to my new pet before going to sleep tonight."

"You have a pet?"

"Yes. I got him a week ago, but we have been so busy I didn't have time to introduce you."

"Well, let's go see..." he caught himself, "go make introductions."

They entered Rani's stone hut and she asked Raja to sit down while she retrieved her new pet.

"What is it?"

"What is *he*," she replied. "Wait and feel."

She went over to a small tank and opened it. Reaching in she picked up some small creature and brought it over to Raja.

"Now open your hand."

He cupped his hands, and felt her place a small furry creature in them. He began to stroke it, pondering what he was holding. It was soft and furry, but had more than four legs. The legs were to the side of its body and seemed long and stringy. He began to count to himself. One, two, three, four, five, ... eight!

"What is he?"

"A tarantula."

Raja tossed the poor little spider away as a pure reflex.

"Ahhh!" The scream was Rani's as she realized her poor little pet had been tossed away. She quickly got down on all fours and began to gently sweep her arms to try to find little Salman, which was his name. Fortunately, it did not take long. Her hand brushed up against Salman, who had not been damaged and was not particularly angry. He landed softly and climbed upon Rani's hands. She then carried him back to his tank safely.

Raja was expecting a scolding, but after a brief moment of silence. There was only laughter, followed by a light slap to his face.

"Go to sleep!" she commanded, and with that he returned, without assistance to his stone hut.

*****

It was a week later when Rani met with Anjali before breakfast. Raja was still asleep.

"How is Raja coping?" asked the concerned Anjali.

"He is much better now, but he still has fits of anger and outrage. I do worry for him so much at times."

"But he is doing better, right? The whole village can feel it."

"Yes, he is better, but I can't help feeling that we robbed him of something precious."

"I understand. Often Jim would privately speak of this 'sight' of his. They treasure it so much."

"It is strange. Raja could never understand us because we do not have sight and the council could never understand him because he did have sight. I wonder if either one is right."

"Probably not, but all you can do is help him to cope."

"*Danyavad*. He has been much better these past few weeks. He can get around fairly well now, even without my help."

"Can I tell you something?"

"*Kya?*"

"It is some advice Jim gave me about Raja many years ago. He told me that Raja has potential, but is held back by his pride, his ego, and rejection of a higher power. Atheists, he said, do not reject God from a sense of justice or knowledge, but of pride. Insecurity makes them want to elevate themselves above all, but only when you humble yourself, only then can you open your ears and hear what others have to say. Remind him of this ... gently. You have to remind him Rani. Your love will get him through it."

"My love, and my prayers."

"Does he know you pray for him?"

"Yes. I used to hide it from him, but he doesn't seem to mind anymore. In fact, I am almost sure I have caught him praying once or twice."

"Who is praying?" The voice belonged to Raja. There had been others passing by, so they did not notice Raja approaching. This itself was an achievement for he normally traipsed around like an elephant, or so Rani used to say. In this instance, he sounded like everyone else, and they were surprised he snuck upon them.

"And to which god are you praying?" he added, somewhat sarcastically.

"We believe all religions are the same," said Rani.

Raja smirked saying, "Yes, they are." Now Rani did not detect the sarcasm in his voice, but Anjali did. Milton had told her much about Raja. While Rani had meant this in a positive way, Raja had intended it in a negative way. She simply could not keep silent. Before discussing the debate which follows however, the atheist reader will be warned that if his tolerance does not extend to those with whom he disagrees, he should skip the next few pages, for Anjali here invalidates his myths about certain religions.

Anjali started simply enough. "The differences in religions are just as important as the similarities. In fact it is what makes Christianity different that first struck me. Most religions are about man seeking God, a noble effort, to be sure, but Christianity is about God reaching out to man. It is not about man reaching up to God, but God reaching down to man. That is why He sent His own Son to die for us."

Raja muttered under his breath, "Yea, a God who kills His kid."

Now Anjali did not react to this, for she had heard it before, but Rani too added her doubts in a more courteous manner.

"Don't be rude Raja!" She then turned back to Anjali, "I must admit, Anjali dear, that I too have never understood the idea of Jesus dying for us."

"I understand Rani. First, Jesus was God. He is called the Son of God because He was not the son of Joseph, but He was God, so He sacrificed His own life, but this doesn't make sense unless you understand the background. I too did not understand for we live in a modern world which is influenced by the western world which ironically is itself an outgrowth of very the Judeo-Christian mindset we do not understand. Please allow me to explain with a story."

"Please do," said Rani.

"Lord, please do not," thought Raja, who oddly called upon the name of the Lord in whom he did not believe at times like these.

"As you know most Hindus do not practice animal sacrifice, and have not for centuries. Except for the Shakta sect and a few others, most of which Jim told me no longer exist, animal sacrifices have long since ceased. Our tradition holds, however, that animal sacrifice was even practiced by the originals settlers here in the valley almost a thousand harvests ago.

"In antiquity, however, not only was animal sacrifice common but human sacrifice is known to have taken place in the most ancient of Egyptian culture, in the old Americas, or so Jim tells me, and most especially in a land called Canaan. The old Canaanite gods, Molech being the worst, were vindictive gods who required the sacrifice of every first born male son.

"One day there was a God fearing man who did not worship Molech, but nevertheless had been raised in that ancient culture. He was taking his son to be sacrificed high up on a sacred mountain top. Just as he was about to strike the knife into his son, the Lord God stayed his hand, and told him that He would provide the sacrifice. The man's name was Abraham and from that day forward no human sacrifice ever took place among his people, who were the forefathers of the Jews, Christians, and Muslims.

"Nearly two thousand years later it is said that a man came who declared that he was that very sacrifice God promised. Although he had been declared innocent by both a Jewish court and by Pontius Pilate, they nevertheless tortured this man to death. Christians believe that we are the ones who deserved to be nailed to that cross for all our sins, but God Himself took the punishment we deserved, so that anyone, regardless of where they were born, whom they had worshipped, or what sins they had once committed, might be saved if they but repent and trust in Him."

Now at this point the atheist may again begin to read, for her "preaching" (or what most people would call explaining in a tolerant discourse of comparative religion) ceased. Raja kept his mouth shut, but oddly was not angered as usual. Rani asked a few more questions, which I will spare the reader, and the conversation soon ended. She had surmised that Christianity teaches that anyone who repents of their sins and turns to Christ can find forgiveness of their sins and go directly to God in heaven upon their death. It was a nice thought, she felt, but she still had her doubts.

Anjali said her "goodbyes" and left Raja and Rani alone.

"Where to today?"

"Today? Nowhere today, but tomorrow I want to take you somewhere special."

"Special? Where?"

"I am not going to tell you, but remember how you told me about something called an 'eclipse'?"

"Yes."

"Well, I am going to take us somewhere where we can feel it when it happens."

"Feel an eclipse?"

"I think so. I have never actually felt one before, but I would like to try."

"Well, I don't see what difference the place makes, but wherever you want to take me is fine."

"Good, it is settled then. Tomorrow I will take you somewhere, but a word of caution. It is dangerous."

"Dangerous?" he was intrigued rather than scared. Almost like a personal challenge.

"Yes, it will take some mountain climbing. Are you up to it?"

"Mountain climbing?" he was astonished. "You do mountain climbing?"

"Yes, we do. Sometimes. We have charted a few paths up on plateaus and mesas, but is dangerous."

To himself he thought, "A blind man rock climbing. Now I will have seen it all," but he said gloatingly, "I live for danger."

"Good. Today, however, is your Hindi lessons. You must learn if you are to live and work here."

"Work?" he was being a little facetious.

"Yes, work! Today's work is school! Are you ready?"

"*Ji haan*," he said with a strong accent in the "n" (which true Indians rarely do).

"Acchaa. Chalo shuru karte hai."

Raja still had no idea what she had said. His Hindi was still horrible, which is ironic since he had actually been born in India and spent his early years there, but He had learned only Tamil. His mother was poor and not well educated, but she was fortunate, for she was a beautiful woman and, having been widowed at an early age, she found an opportunity to marry an Indian of some means who took a job in America. He had literally seen both sides of life. His youth was spent in a small village in the south of India but by age eight he was living in an upper middle class home in Irving, Texas, USA. He had a good education thereafter and went to the University of Texas to receive his Bachelors and Masters in earth sciences. He received his Ph.D. from Baylor University, which is where he had first met James Milton. From these experiences he had learned Tamil, English, and French, but no Hindi.

The truth is Raja was a little reluctant to let anyone know how much Hindi he had learned and how much he could understand. He knew Pita-ji would put him to work someday, and he wished to delay that day as much as possible. As long as Rani was teaching him how to speak Hindi and showing him (or rather "guiding" him) around the village he was happy. The truth is he was far happier than he would ever let anyone know. He did not want them to forget what they had done to him, and he was still bitter, but these past few months were actually months that he had enjoyed more than any in his life. It was because, for the first time in his life, he was truly in love.

"Shall we begin?"

*****

It was early morning when they set out. Raja thought it was crazy for a blind man to go mountain climbing, but he was sure Rani knew what she was doing. Of course there was some communication failure as well. He was delighted to find that they did not actually need mountain climbing gear, which meant that her understanding of mountain climbing was not as rigorous as his. Whatever they were doing would include hands and feet, but nothing else. Perhaps it would not be as dangerous as he had thought. It was thirty minutes before they reached the base of a plateau.

"Here is the base. Let me feel around for the marker and make sure we are at the right mesa."

She walked up against a cliff and started to feel around. She moved to a corner, and then took two steps to the right. Finally her hand came to rest upon carved words. They had chiseled words into the rock. They read "*Swargyea Taraye*" in their Braille style script. This is translated, "Plateau of the Heavens."

"This is it. Just give me a minute to remember where the trail begins."

Raja was intrigued. "There is a trail?"

"Well, sort of. It is still quite dangerous. We will have to crawl on all fours so don't be in a hurry. If you try to climb up on two feet and fall, you could fall off the edge and to your death."

"I see."

"No, you don't." She paused to think for a moment. "You wouldn't leave me here all alone would you?"

"What? No. I promise I won't purposely jump to my death, if that is what you mean." Raja was a little depressed at the insinuation, but he knew she was right. He had already tried to kill himself once, and thought about it many times.

"Promise?"

"Yes. I promise."

"*Acchaa*. Wait."

She moved around the corner of the plateau, tripping once as it was not familiar territory for her. Raja laughed, but at the same time thought nervously, "If she fell down here, what happens if she falls on the mountain?" Surely she knew what she was doing.

"Here! *Aao!*" she cried.

He moved toward the sound of her voice, tripping twice.

"It is okay. Take it slow, my Raja," she warned.

"Now she tells me," he thought to himself. She was excited; nothing else.

"We came early in the morning so that we can take our time. It is a long hike and we must crawl on all fours so that we won't fall. It is a long way down."

"But there is a trail?" he reiterated.

"Of sorts, yes."

"Of sorts?" he thought to himself.

"Now follow me closely. Anytime you need to rest, please do so. Feel with your hands before you take a step and make sure the ground is solid. There are lots of loose rocks."

"Why are we doing this?"

"You don't want to come? We can go back."

"No no no. I want to come." He figured she was bluffing, but he didn't want to take any chances. Curiosity had gotten the better of him, as Rani had hoped. She was afraid that he might not want to come since he had constantly protested "what is the point if I can't see" this or that. Nevertheless, although he liked to complain (it was a way of letting her know his pain) he was beginning to enjoy their excursions for more than Rani's company. He had gotten to love the secret waterfall hideaway in particular.

"Follow me. To the left at the big rock," she said. Her instructions were constant and reassuring. The path was not particularly steep but it was winding. Raja wondered how they had found this path in the first place, but then he remembered that they had been here for a thousand years. The people had doubtless explored every corner of the valley and every possible entrance and exit (of which there was only one). Still, there must be something special about the plateau, he reasoned.

Almost an hour had passed and they had brought no water with them. It was not a hot day at all, but a cool one. Nevertheless, it was rather strenuous. When he inquired about water, Rani assured him that there was a small pool at the top which they should reach in fifteen minutes or less.

The wind whistled and pressed against Raja's back. It often made climbers, particularly inexperienced ones, nervous for it led to an unconscious fear that the wind would make him loose balance and fall. When he was up far above everything else, his eyes told him something was wrong. His mind said that he should not be so far above the ground. This is what causes vertigo. It is a fear of falling when the mind interprets unique circumstances. Raja, of course, gained control over his mind and was not particularly afraid of heights, but the sensations were quite different without eyesight. He was actually more brave, and yet he could *feel*, yes "feel", how high up they were. The wind told him that. The sounds of birds chirping from far below also told his mind that they were very far up. Had he still had eyes, he would doubtless have closed them.

"Are you ready to finish? Just another fifteen minutes," urged Rani.

"I am ready and eager."

In fact, it was only ten minutes. They had reached the top, but Raja was still crawling on all fours. Rani could hear his scurrying and told him, "Here. We are at the top now. Come over here to the pool and refreshen yourself."

Indeed, it was refreshing. The water was very cool and pure. All the water in the valley was clean. It had come from pure rainwater and melted snow. True, he missed caffeine, but he was in better shape now than he had been when he entered the valley.

"Here now," Rani said, "Come this way?"

"Where are we going now?"

"Just to the edge over here."

"The edge?" he replied a little nervously.

Rani laughed a little. "Yes. Don't worry. *Main hoon*."

He walked over to the sound of her voice and bumped into her extended hand, which he took. Their fingers intertwined and she led him a few feet until her own feet touched a small row of rocks.

"Here is the warning track. Now do as I do."

"What?"

She stepped over the rocks and then squatted down, "Get down on your knees with me."

He did so.

"Now sit on your rear and scoot with me."

Raja felt silly, like a dog cleaning his backside, but he did so. As they scooted closer to the edge Raja could hear the wind whistling over the ledge. Once his feet no longer felt earth, he sensed he was at the cliff's edge.

"Now, be careful. Hold on to me, and use the cliff as your would a chair." She held on tightly, lest he fall, but he was far more scared than her. This was, after all, the first time he had ever done such a thing.

"Are you sure you know what you are doing?" he asked.

"Do you trust me?"

"Yes."

"Do you believe me?"

"Yes."

"Then walk by faith, not by your sight."

Raja knew he had heard that somewhere before, but he wasn't quite sure where. In any case, it gave new meaning to the saying. It was not the blind leading the blind. It was not blind faith. It was simply trusting in someone who knows what is best, and Raja trusted Rani despite everything; perhaps even because of it. Finally, his legs dropped down and there he sat, on cliff's edge with the wind hitting his back.

Rani spoke gently. "We come here sometimes to worship. You can feel the whole valley up here. The wind at your back, and swirling at your feet. You can hear the echoes of the birds and the sound of the wind in the canyons. It is truly beautiful."

"I am beginning to understand. There are so many simple pleasures I never noticed before. I guess my eyes blinded me to much of the world around me," he answered.

Rani extends her hands, with her palms up, and says, "Do you feel that?"

"What?"

She reaches over and grabs his hand, turning his palms upwards, and lifting them to the sky. "That. The warmth of the sun."

"Oh, yes. I do."

"You feel it, but could you actually see it before?"

Raja pauses for a second to think. He had never really even thought about it that way. "Sort of," is all he could say.

"Sort of?"

"Well, I guess the truth is that just associated certain sights and colors with heat, but it is not *really* something you see. It is something you feel."

"You don't have to see it to know it is real. You know it is real by what it does. You can feel it. You can sense it. Like love."

"Love ... Love. You know, I have never really felt love before. Sex, yes, but not love."

It is perhaps a good thing that Raja could not see the expression on Rani's face, for she was not thrilled to hear his confession, but Raja was still thinking aloud.

"Not until now," he finished.

Rani changed the subject, not realizing the heart felt confession that Raja had just made. "I wonder if we can feel that eclipse."

"I don't know how you could feel it."

"But you said before you can't see heat. You feel it, so will not the earth become cold when there is an eclipse?"

It was a fair question, but the answer was, "No no, the sun is so huge and it is only blocked for less than a minute, so I doubt you will be able to sense the difference anymore than you do if clouds pass by."

"We can feel cloudy days."

This seemed a little suspect to Raja, although he was beginning to believe almost anything, but could she really feel an eclipse? Probably not, but he didn't care anymore. He decided he would play along if and when she said she felt such a thing.

"Is it happening now?" she finally asks.

"Must be," he responded, and with that she jumped up from the cliffs edge and ran back toward the small pool with her hands sticking up toward the sky. Raja was a little unnerved as he knew he was still sitting on the edge of a precipice and teetering upon death should he fall. He slowly scooted backwards and stood up. As he walked toward Rani he stumbled upon the warning track, for he still had not gotten used to walking lightly as Rani said.

Rani heard him approach and spoke gently. "I am here. Can you feel it?"

Raja did not even lift his hands, but replied, "Yes. Yes I can."

"Tell me what it looks like, please."

"The sun is blocked by the moon. It is dark as night right now. There is no light."

Rani did not fully understand, "but I can still feel heat. Are you sure it isn't still there?"

"It is still there, yes. You just can't see it."

"It is there, but you cannot see it?"

"Yes, I can't see it, but I can still feel it. Like the beat of your heart."

A broad smiled crossed her lips, and she moved her hands from the sky to Raja's face. "You are learning." She felt his face. He instinctively started to pull back, but resisted the urge and let her run her fingers over his face. "You have never been in love before?"

"No. Never."

"Could you not see love?"

Laughing to himself, "no."

"Could you put it in a laboratory?"

"No."

"Could you not feel it and know it is real?"

"No. Not before." He took hold of her hands. "I want to make a confession to you."

"You mean about the sex?" her voice almost broke.

"No," he fought off the urge to laugh. "About my soul."

Rani perked up. If he was talking about his soul, then he was talking religion, whether he knew it or not. Was he beginning to understand?

"I think I understand now what John Newton meant. I had never understood it before."

"Who?"

"He was a slave trader who became a Christian convert and led the abolitionist movement against slavery. He wrote some religious song I used to think was utter nonsense. Now I think I understand."

"*Bolo*. Tell me. What was it?"

He hummed it softly, trying to remember the words. He was no singer, but he almost whispered the song.

"Amazing Grace, how sweet the sound,
"That saved a wretch like me....
"I once was lost but now am found,
"Was blind, but now, I see."

"He was blind, but gained sight?" Rani did not understand, but Raja did.

He was oblivious to her words, and continued speaking. "That is what Milton used to try to tell me. Funny really. I had everything and could see nothing. I enjoyed nothing. I loved nothing. Then God took everything away from me. I lost everything and now I see all the things I could never see before. I smell the flowers, I feel the warmth of the sun, the softness of your touch, the gentle breeze. Most of all, I feel the love I never knew. I know now what it was Milton wanted me to understand." His last words could not be heard, for they came so softly that only a lip reader would know that he said. "You were wrong about me Milton. I am a part now."

Rani did not fully understand what had happened, but she didn't care. She knew only that Raja was a changed man. That was something most women dream of doing, but their dreams all turn to nightmares. When women seek to change a bad men, the man realizes it and plays a game, for bad men see relationships as a game; nothing more. God knows how many women have wasted years of their lives hoping to do what only the Lord can do: change a sinful heart. Rani was fortunate, but she knew in her heart that she had not changed him. It was God who was changing him, and God still had work to do, as He does with us all.

Their hands were now firmly placed on each other's face, and their lips moved closer and closer to one another. For the first time they kissed. It was an innocent kiss. It was not a sensuous or sexual one, but a simple innocent one, and that made it all the more special.

I believe in the sun even when it is not shining
I believe in love even when I am alone
I believe in God even when He is silent

The LORD opens the eyes of the blind;
The LORD raises up those who have fallen;
For whoever calls on the name of the LORD
will be saved

... (Psalm 146:8 & Romans 10:13)